He didn't mix business with pleasure

"How many jobs were you short-listed for, Miss Peters, before you found one where your immediate superior was a bachelor?" he asked brusquely, his glance on her wide green eyes.

Kacie's jaw dropped. She fought to remain cool. Before she could reply, Elliot Quantrell went on.

"We both know what goes on inside your devious mind, so please get this straight. You're here to work, and work only. Got it?"

"You're suggesting," she asked, "that I might . . . might have it in mind to do something about your being a bachelor?"

"I've experience of your sort," he cut in harshly.

There was no civil way to continue the conversation. Kacie seethed from his offensive remarks, yet wondered why it entered her soul to want his approval.

Jessica Steele first tried her hand at writing
romance novels at her husband's encouragement two
years after they were married. She fondly remembers
the day her first novel was accepted for publication.
"Peter mopped me up, and neither of us cooked that
night," she recalls. "We went out to dinner." She and
her husband live in a hundred-year-old cottage in
Worcestershire, and they've traveled to many
fascinating places—such as China, Japan, Mexico
and Denmark—that make wonderful settings for
her books.

Books by Jessica Steele

HARLEQUIN ROMANCE
2494—BUT KNOW NOT WHY
2502—DISHONEST WOMAN
2555—DISTRUST HER SHADOW
2580—TETHERED LIBERTY
2607—TOMORROW—COME SOON
2687—NO HONOURABLE COMPROMISE
2789—MISLEADING ENCOUNTER

HARLEQUIN PRESENTS
717—RUTHLESS IN ALL
725—GALLANT ANTAGONIST
749—BOND OF VENGEANCE
766—NO HOLDS BARRED
767—FACADE
836—A PROMISE TO DISHONOUR

These books may be available at your local bookseller.

Don't miss any of our special offers. Write to us at the
following address for information on our newest releases.

Harlequin Reader Service
901 Fuhrmann Blvd., P.O. Box 1397, Buffalo, NY 14240
Canadian address: P.O. Box 603,
Fort Erie, Ont. L2A 9Z9

So Near, So Far

Jessica Steele

Harlequin Books

TORONTO • NEW YORK • LONDON
AMSTERDAM • PARIS • SYDNEY • HAMBURG
STOCKHOLM • ATHENS • TOKYO • MILAN

Original hardcover edition published in 1986
by Mills & Boon Limited

ISBN 0-373-02800-8

Harlequin Romance first edition November 1986

CHAPTER ONE

FEBRUARY, Kacie thought, as she stared despondently at the warming bars of her gas fire that Sunday afternoon, was truly the bleakest month of the year. Not, she honestly admitted, that she could put the blame for the way she was feeling solely down to the weather.

Nobody had asked her to give up her job at the end of last month. Vincent Jenner, her ex-boss, had been little short of appalled when, carrying through a resolution made with the new year, she had, on the second of January, given in her notice.

'But—why?' he had asked astonished. 'Is it something I've done? Something I've said?' And, with panic which would have been flattering had her reason for telling him she wanted to leave not been so painful, 'If it's money, Kacie, you've only to name . . .'

'It's nothing like that,' she had quickly replied, and had averted her eyes from his dear kind face to tell him of the half truth, half fabrication she had decided upon. Even so, a great deal of tact was needed when, reminding him of how she had spent her Christmas holiday with her mother and stepfather, she went on, 'I think I may have mentioned at some time the hard struggle my mother had in her determination I should receive the best business training money could buy.'

'I knew things were a bit tight before she re-married,' Vincent agreed, his face sombre.

'I can only ever remember being well turned out,' Kacie told him. 'But it was brought home to me that "tight" was an understatement when, over Christmas,

my mother made some laughing reference to when
William was courting her, how each time he took her out
she would worry that she had to wear the same old dress.'

Vincent had started to look perplexed, not really
understanding what any of this had to do with Kacie
giving in her notice. 'You're saying she couldn't afford
a new dress.' He went along with her.

Kacie had promised herself she would not be
emotional at this interview. But when she thought of
the sacrifices her mother had made, a lump came to
her throat.

'For herself, she couldn't afford anything new.' She
swallowed to tell him. 'Every penny she had was spent
on my education, my text books, my clothes, and
anything else she thought would have been my right
had my father been alive.'

His confusion was none the clearer. 'You've certainly
repaid her belief in your ability,' Vincent said warmly,
'You're way and above the best secretary I've ever
had—without stretching yourself too.'

Like manna from heaven, Kacie grabbed at the
opening he had unwittingly given her. 'Which is why I
must leave,' she told him. 'I should be *stretching*
myself. I feel I owe it not only to myself, but also to
my mother, for all the sacrifices she made, that I
should make more of my career.' Swiftly, while she
still had sufficient strength of will, she told him, 'I've
applied for the position of personal and confidential
secretary to the chairman of Quantrell Industries.'

A small explosive pop from the gas fire brought
Kacie out from her reverie. Her thoughts returned to
Vincent. He had been hurt and upset, and had tried to
coax her out of her decision, but she had discovered an
inherited determination which, coupled with the
memory of how she had agonised the day before in
reaching her decision, had made her adamant.

Kacie supposed being in her mother's company for longer than the usual brief weekend, must have something to do with the realisation she had better take some action. Although the holiday had passed without her mother making the smallest reference to the values she had tried to imbue in her as a child, something must have rubbed off. Because it had been on that drive from the Warwickshire village of Wellsingham that Kacie had decided that it just was not right she should spend any more of her life in languishing after a married man.

Not that Vincent had any idea of how she felt about him. It had not dawned on Kacie herself until about six months ago that the warm sympathy she had for him, and his problems, was love. She had worked for Vincent for three years, and was aware he was fond of her. It had, however, taken that extended Christmas break in her mother's home to show her that, even if Vincent did love her, nothing could come of it while he was still married to Julie—turbulent though that marriage might be.

On New Year's Day Kacie had returned to her London flat, to spend the rest of the day coming to a painful conclusion. She wanted to be more to Vincent than the sympathetic ear she had been on the occasions when Julie walked out on him; but since Julie always came back—which had to mean they must in some peculiar fashion still be in love with each other—Kacie saw she had better change her job.

She had been wrapping up some rubbish in the Christmas Eve edition of a newspaper that evening, when the advert for a personal and confidential secretary to the chairman of Quantrell Industries had jumped out at her. Her application was posted and the die cast. She had been called for a first, and then for a second interview.

Not that she had been interviewed by the chairman himself. Elliot Quantrell was out of the country and would not be back until mid-February. One of his directors sat in at the second interview, and although she had not cared for the leering light she saw in the eyes of the balding Cecil Glover, she supposed she had him to thank—along with the excellent reference Vincent, despite his hurt feelings, had given her—that she had landed the job to start on the first of February.

That was two weeks ago, she reflected, as she left her seat by the gas fire and went to the kitchen to make herself a cup of coffee. Tomorrow, she would meet her boss for the first time.

She wondered if she would like Elliot Quantrell. Would it matter if she didn't? She had already learned he was always so here, there and everywhere, that one had to glue his feet to the floor if you wanted him to stay in one place for any length of time!

Simon Fletcher, ringing her from the badminton club to ask her to join him for a game, broke her train of thought. In her opinion, Simon ate, slept and dreamed badminton.

'The tournament will soon be here,' he pressed, refusing to be put off when she invented the excuse of having masses to do. 'We can do with all the practice we can get if we're to walk away with the mixed doubles cup.'

'Isn't Sue there?' she tried. 'She'll give you a game if . . .'

'I know that,' he answered, starting to sound aggrieved. He didn't realise that Susan Baylis had a crush on him. 'But she's only the reserve. *You*,' he stressed, 'are my partner!'

When Kacie put down the phone she wondered how on earth she had let herself get roped in for the tournament. Popular with both sexes, she had only joined the club as an alternative to dating men who, in her experience, wanted to get serious after a few dates.

Being sensitive to emotional blackmail got you nowhere, she thought, as she left her flat. It was not as if she fancied a game tonight. Yet here she was, with the rain tipping down, getting her car out and going to the club.

For the most part, Kacie was even-tempered, and had a face and figure which many girls would give their eye teeth for. But since no one should know of her inner unhappiness, she was at pains to appear the same outwardly friendly and cheerful person she had been before she had cut Vincent Jenner out of her life.

She was buttonholed by several male members in turn when she entered the club. But even if she had to invent a few excuses for why she did not have a free evening the following week, Kacie owned that it had done her good to get out. There was no time for disconsolate thoughts when chasing a shuttlecock around.

Simon Fletcher had been all smiles, she mused, when she let herself back into her flat. Sue Baylis had been all shiny-eyed too, when Simon had taken his mind off badminton to carelessly offer, 'I'm going your way, Sue, if you want a lift.'

Perhaps I should get out more, Kacie considered, as she showered and then climbed into bed. Though, when she thought about it, none of the men at the club, nice as they were, were scintillating enough to make her really want to clamber out of her safe little rut.

Kacie lay down and concentrated her thoughts on the coming day. She had found enough to do at Quantrell Industries, but the work so far had been easily within her capabilities. She supposed she had worked too hard at obtaining her qualifications for it to be anything other. But tomorrow, she would meet the man himself, and had heard it said that he worked like a Trojan, and expected everyone near to do likewise.

Which was all right by her. Maybe if she had something to really get her teeth into, it would give her less time to wonder what Vincent was doing.

Deliberately she switched her thoughts away from Vincent and his sincere parting words and promise to keep in touch. Instead she reflected on her second interview for the job at Quantrell's. Mr Owens, the personnel manager had hummed and hawed, she remembered, so much so that she had begun to think her chances of getting the job were nil. But then Cecil Glover had chipped in to say in his view, with her qualifications and the glowing reference from her present employer, there was no one more suitable than Miss Peters on their short list.

In reliving that interview, Kacie remembered the crass answer she had given in reply to the director's enquiry of, 'And now, my dear, is there anything more you would like to ask us?'

Kacie suspected there were moments in everyone's life when they looked back and cringed at their own idiocy. But, with an image of Vincent brought to mind by Cecil Glover's previous question, and the director's off-putting leer not being conducive to collected thought, the question she asked was:

'Is Mr Quantrell married?'

Fortunately, neither of her interviewers appeared to think her question as ridiculous as she did. As if it was commonplace for nervous candidates to ask totally irrelevant questions, she was told that the chairman was a bachelor. She then learned that if she accepted the position, she would be thrown in at the deep end, because Mr Qauntrell's present secretary was with him in Canada and was staying on in their Canadian division in an administrative role.

Her predecessor must have excelled to warrant such promotion, and Kacie was aware she was likely to be kept on her toes when Elliot Quantrell returned. That did not worry her. Instead, since she herself had opted to go higher in her career, it seemed that there was every prospect for a career minded female to climb the executive ladder within the organisation.

Monday dawned as bleak as the day before. Determined to make a good impression at her first meeting with Elliot Quantrell, Kacie pushed aside thoughts that she would by far prefer to make her way to Vincent's office.

The thought crossed her mind that, this being the chairman's first day back, he might call on other offices on the way in. It occurred to her it could well be midday before she made his acquaintance. Nevertheless Kacie, dressed in a smart suit of pale grey, which although tailored could not conceal her femininity, was at her desk well before she needed to be.

When, on the stroke of nine, the office door was opened by a tall, dark-haired man somewhere in his middle thirties, she knew she was not going to have to wait until midday to meet the chairman. Elliot Quantrell had arrived!

She knew it the minute she clapped eyes on him. He extended an aura of energy and drive which seemed to step into the office with him.

But the cordial greeting she had ready did not make it past her lips, because suddenly, as he took a pace towards her, he froze. Before she could even open her mouth—the jut of his hard jaw told her he was not impressed by the creamy-complexioned redhead in his sight and effectively silenced her—Elliot Quantrell got in first.

'*Who*—are you?' he asked, his words clipped, curt.

'I'm Kacie Peters, your new secretary,' she replied. 'I . . .' The look of total outrage which came to his face halted her. Though she had been going to add more, he did not give her the chance.

'The hell—you are,' he said grimly and, furious, he strode out again leaving her gaping and speechless.

Her green eyes widened at this inauspicious start to what she had hoped would be a harmonious working relationship and suddenly she became aware of how, within the first minute of meeting him, her adrenalin had started to pump.

My God, she thought, her usually even temperament tilted to feel anger, what a man!

Ten minutes later, the stirring of anger she had felt at his rudeness had quieted down, but she was still no nearer to comprehending what it was about her that Elliot Quantrell had taken exception to.

She heard him enter his office through the next door down in the corridor. Two seconds later his voice came over the intercom with the terse order, 'Get in here.' Kacie took up her note pad and pencil and headed for the communicating door. Judging from his tone, she had an idea that she would soon know what it was about her that he did not like.

Elliot Quantrell was studying a file when she went into his office. Without raising his eyes from the matter that absorbed his attention, he motioned her to take the chair at the side of his desk.

Kacie settled herself on the chair, and glanced at him. Her eyes then flicked to the cover of the file in his hands and, without disquiet, noted he must have been down to personnel. The file he held was labelled with her name.

Thorough, she thought, must be his middle name. Not one word came from him until he had read every note, comment, and remark her file contained; right from her first letter of application to the copy of the letter from Mr Owens which had formally offered her the job.

Then with a movement so swift that Kacie knew she would do well to keep her wits about her, he tossed the file to one side while at the same time, he fired, 'How old are you?'

Why he had to ask that when all that sort of information was there in the file he had just read, was beyond her. But even as her adrenalin started to pump a second time, Kacie managed to retain a composed look and reply levelly, 'Twenty-four.'

Cold grey eyes bored into her, but whatever thoughts were going on behind his detailed scrutiny were carefully veiled. She was totally unprepared, therefore, for his aggressive disbelief when, his scrutiny of her over, he rapped, 'Let's have the truth.'

'The truth?' she queried. 'You mean—about my age?'

His overbearing manner had ruffled her even temperament again. She was tempted to offer a tart, 'I'll see you have sight of my birth certificate,' when shortly, he said, 'Leaving aside the fact that you don't look twenty, you surely don't expect me to swallow that, at twenty-four, you decided to leave a tin-pot firm like Jenner Products for no other reason than that of "advancement"?'

To have him describe Vincent's firm in such derogatory terms, made her anger flare. Though it gave her a slightly breathless feeling that this pig of a man had wasted no time to look beyond the 'wanting advancement' excuse she had given for leaving Jenner Products.

'I've already given a sound reason.' She held down her anger and emotion, her pride insisting that no one should know the real reason for her leaving Vincent's firm. 'My career with Jenner Products was leading nowhere. It was with the intention of advancing myself that I . . .'

'You were Vincent Jenner's secretary for three years,' he cut in harshly. 'Are you trying to tell me it took all of three years for it to dawn on you that being Jenner's secretary was as high as you were likely to go with that company?'

He had a point there, she had to admit it. She also had to admit that, while she had found her work for Vincent pleasant and undemanding, she had held no particular aspirations for her career.

'I had known for some time, naturally,' she replied. 'But, since I'd had two previous jobs before I came to London to work for Mr Jenner, I thought, from a future employer's point of view, it might be better if I could show I didn't swap employers every five minutes, but could show I'd stayed with the same employer for a number of years.'

He was unimpressed, she could see that. She had already been through two interviews, but it seemed she was about to be put through a third, and far more rigorous one. Kacie fought to remain cool, but very nearly crumpled when without warning, as if there was not a thing he was not aware of, Elliot Quantrell suddenly shot at her, 'That Jenner is a married man had nothing to do with your decision to give notice, did it?'

Incredulous and unsure that her jaw had not momentarily dropped, Kacie realised that she had never before met a man who had such an insidious ability for homing straight to the root of the matter. As she battled to get herself together she saw that it

was only by being positive that she had not managed
to give away even the tiniest clue and that all Elliot
Quantrell had to go on was mere guesswork.

'I'm afraid, Mr Quantrell,' she told him coldly,
uncaring that his eyes had narrowed at her tone, 'I
don't understand your question.'

His jaw jutted an aggressive fraction, but she was
quite unprepared when, his scepticism rife, the gloves
well and truly came off. She was absolutely dumbfounded to hear what conclusions the chairman of
Quantrell Industries had drawn from reading the
contents of her personnel file.

'How many jobs were you short listed for, Miss
Peters,' he asked, his voice glacial, 'before you found
one where your immediate superior was a bachelor?'

Her jaw definitely dropped then. She was fast
realising that Mr Owens must have jotted down
everything, including that inane question about Mr
Quantrell's marital status during her second interview.

Elliot Quantrell did not wait for her to answer, but
went steamrollering on, 'We both know exactly what
goes on inside your devious little mind, so we'll have
it straight before we go any further. You are here to
work, and work only. I'm not the remotest bit
interested in mixing business with pleasure,' he
stressed heavily. 'Which means—if I catch you so
much as giving me the merest coy glance, out you go.
Got it?'

For several long, winded moments, Kacie was
incapable of speech. When all her adult life she'd had
trouble in keeping the opposite sex at arm's length—to
hear Elliot Quantrell *actually* warn her off amazed her!

When she did find the breath to reply, she could not
keep her amazement hidden, or keep hold of the cool
manner she had been at pains to present. 'You're
suggesting,' she asked, her eyes large in her face, 'I

might—might have it in mind to do something about you being a bachelor?'

'I've already warned you about the coy look,' he threatened, his glance on her wide green eyes.

'Coy!' Kacie exclaimed, certain she had never looked coy in her life. 'My God!' she suddenly exploded, 'You must have met some peculiar women in your . . .'

'I've experience of your sort, Miss Peters,' he cut in harshly.

'Oh, I see,' she mumbled, her flare of temper dying as suddenly as it had been born.

'Precisely what do you see?' he rapped shortly.

'Nothing, except that you've recently had secretary trouble—er—in that direction,' she murmured. Then she heard, though only because he was underlining the way it was to be, that she had nearly hit the nail on the head.

'Not recently,' he informed her icily. 'I was inexperienced enough when I was getting started to see no harm in dating my secretary a couple of times, experience came the hard way, when instead of accepting the relationship outside the office had run its course, she not only left me high and dry, but went to work for a company who were competing for the same contracts.'

'You're saying—she told them about . . .'

'Within her first day there wasn't a thing confidential to this office which my competitors didn't know about,' he gritted. 'It set me back a whole year.'

What he had just said was truly dreadful. But just the same, Kacie could not help but feel niggled. It was bad enough to be accused of wanting to get her hooks into Elliot Quantrell, without him warning her off, but that he should put her in the same class as that disloyal secretary, just as if he thought she too would have no qualms about handing over confidential matter to the opposition, was a bit much, she thought.

'If you feel like that about women secretaries,' she said, her tone cold again as it came to her that this job didn't look as though it was going to last much longer than her first morning with him anyway, 'it's a wonder to me you continue to employ secretaries of the female sex at all.'

Kacie reckoned that there would be no derogatory answer he could give to that comment but she was stunned when, before she could blink, back came the answer. 'For myself, I don't.' And while she was gaping afresh. 'I thought Owens knew that without my having to stress the fact,' he said tightly.

'You were expecting a male to be sitting—where I was sitting—when you walked in!' she gasped.

'Even with a telephoned conversation with Cecil Glover that was distorted by atmospherics, I was confident I'd find a Peter Something-or-other in that chair this morning.'

Stumped to know what to reply to that, and feeling her hold on the prized job of secretary to the chairman of Quantrell Industries slipping more and more all the time, Kacie murmured, 'Mr Glover was present at my second interview.'

'That,' replied Elliot Quantrell tersely, scanning his eyes over her features, 'explains a lot.' Then, while Kacie was wondering if, to save face, she should leave her seat and go before he could conclude this interview by telling her she was not suitable for the job, he reached for the nearest bundle of paper work, and curtly, he commanded, 'Take a letter.'

When had she ever imagined she liked hard work? Kacie wondered as she reeled into the car-park that night. Slavery was more the term she would have used for the way she had been run off her ball point that day. What a day, she thought as she collapsed into her car. What a man! Oh, where was her bed!

When later that night Kacie eventually made it to her bed, she lay there to realise firstly, that when she had told Vincent she thought she should be stretching herself, she'd had no idea that would mean she would be going flat out as she had been ever since Elliot Quantrell had said those immortal words, 'Take a letter'.

Her second realisation was that this was the first time since her introduction to Elliot Quantrell, that Vincent had crept to the periphery of her thinking.

Kacie closed her eyes, but, strangely, it was not Vincent who filled her last waking thought. Memory filtered in of how she had wondered if she would like her new boss when she met him. But, it had appeared during a day that at one and the same time had seemed never ending and yet had flashed by, that her likes and dislikes did not come into it. For, in Elliot Quantrell's bossy world, whether his secretary liked him or not, was entirely immaterial.

CHAPTER TWO

REFRESHED from a sound sleep, Kacie felt ready to tackle anything when she drove to the office the next day.

With Elliot Quantrell, blunt, curt, and obviously hating her like poison, working at a pace which left her without a chance to take a breather, she was never more pleased to suddenly discover it was lunch time.

Not that she had any idea what time it was until Mike Carey brought her in some figures which the chairman had ordered to be on his desk by two. Many times during the previous fortnight she had been obliged to tactfully brush off Mike Carey's attempts to date her. So she was not entirely fooled when, after a glance to his watch, he should feign surprise, and exclaim: 'Only two minutes to lunch!'

About to avert an invitation out to lunch, Kacie then saw, whereas Mike could not, that Elliot Quantrell had come to stand in his office doorway. His expression was far from ecstatic when he caught sight of the young accountant chatting up his secretary, but Kacie had no chance to tip Mike off.

Giving her the full benefit of his charm, he—as though the idea had just come to him—was already asking, 'How about joining me for a crust?'

'Your timing's too obvious, Carey,' came the sharp, authoritative voice, before she could make any reply. While Mike spun round as though shot, Elliot Quantrell strode forward, and with an abrasive, 'Are those my figures?' to Kacie, he took them from her hand, and strode back into his office.

'Perhaps some other time, Mike,' Kacie murmured, the best she could do to salve any wounded pride. 'I've some shopping to do this lunch time.'

Her flagging energy was revived by a sandwich and a cup of coffee. She returned to her place of work to wonder if her employer had been hard at it all through the lunch hour, for before she had even so much as stowed away her bag, the voice she was beginning to hate commanded, 'I want you in here.' Kacie went, once again, into overdrive.

At four o'clock Elliot Quantrell went out on some errand, and with a thankful sigh, Kacie stretched her cramped muscles.

At five-past four the phone rang—it had seemed to ring non-stop for most of the day. This time it was not a business call, but Angus Macdonald, a co-member of her badminton club. Angus had been trying without success to contact Babs Ellwell, another member, and asked would Kacie pass on the message that although he was having car trouble and would be late, he would definitely be at the club that night.

'You are going tonight?' he asked as an afterthought.

If Kacie's thoughts had been on going anywhere, it was to an early bed. But, even as she wondered where she was going to summon the energy from, she thought of Simon Fletcher fretting himself into a panic if she was not there for a practice game, and so confirmed, 'I'll be there.'

A happy Angus then remarked how fortunate it was he had remembered her recent change of work place, and Kacie was just about to terminate the conversation, when Elliot Quantrell returned.

'I'll see you later tonight, Angus,' she said, and looked up to receive a cold look from her employer as he strode past her desk and into his own office.

By the end of that first week of the chairman being

back in harness, Kacie had just about had enough of him. As far as she was concerned, the sooner he took himself off to another part of his empire the better—preferably, the most distant part.

She sighed when she recalled that according to his desk diary, apart from a return trip to Canada, which was all of a couple of months away, he had nothing else booked. It appeared she was stuck with him!

More than once she contemplated giving in her notice. Wednesday, in particular, had been a day when, more terse than usual in his barked orders, he had goaded what she had always thought of as her placid temperament. Then, she had nearly told him what he could do with his job. But she had not and in spite of the gut feeling she had that he was only waiting his chance to dismiss her, a whole week had passed, and she was still there.

She pondered why he had not told her to go and to never come back. Did he perhaps have a streak of fairness in him which, while her work came up to scratch, compelled him to put up with the fact she was a female? Quickly she saw it had nothing to do with him being fair minded. All that motivated him was self-consideration; because if he gave her the push, he could well find himself without a slave at his beck and call for weeks while he waited for personnel to come up with the more suitable *male* secretary.

With two free days before her, Kacie felt an urge to spend the weekend in the company of two people who loved her most—her mother and William. But the memory of Simon Fletcher and his near paranoia about the impending tournament intruded.

Aware of her commitment to put in a couple of appearances at the club over the weekend, she began to wish she had never joined the club, let alone agreed to partner Simon.

Unable to visit Wellsingham, Kacie did the next best thing, and spoke with her mother on the phone. No sooner were greetings out of the way, than her mother remembered, 'Mr Quantrell was due back last Monday, wasn't he?' Her pride was unmistakable that her daughter was working in the prized job of his personal secretary. 'How are you getting on with him?' she asked.

In view of her mother's pride in her achievement, Kacie hesitated, though tempted to tell her mother what a swine he was.

'I—haven't had much time to find out,' she hedged. 'He's a demon for work, so naturally there's been no time for personalities to enter into it.'

'He'll have had masses to catch up on, having been out of the country for so long,' Rosa Harding replied, her pleasure in her daughter's achievement once again apparent. 'Though I'm sure you've done everything to help him.'

'It's—been—quite a week,' Kacie murmured, and as soon as she could, she got her mother off the subject.

For a full five minutes after she came from the phone, Kacie was in deep thought. The memory of the congratulations when word had got round the club about her new job crowded in on her recollection. She remembered too Vincent's reluctance to see her go and how he had appeared somewhat appeased that she was leaving him for a much more exalted position. She had known without that phone call just now, how proud her mother and William had been when she had been able to tell them that she had actually been offered the job. Even her mother's daily help had shown delight in the news; which meant it was quite likely the whole of Wellsingham now knew what a very clever daughter Mrs Harding had.

Some minutes later, Kacie had put it all together

and had seen that even though she might feel like walking out next week, like she had every day this past week, there was no way now she could do so. How could she? Apart from the feeling she would be letting everyone down, she had to consider her mother who had sacrificed so much for her. It was small return to allow her mother to experience that pride for as long as she could.

Kacie was glum when she thought of Elliot Quantrell and his manner with her all last week. With a start of surprise, she suddenly realised that, even though he had worked the socks off her, never, not for one moment, had she been bored! Working with Elliot Quantrell was far more stimulating than her work with Vincent had ever been! Kacie thought it about time she went and got out her badminton gear.

But going to the club did not put Elliot Quantrell out of her head, and she went to bed on Sunday having come to the view that she was going to have to put up with him and his uncivil manner. It was unthinkable she should tell anyone, especially her mother, that her job with Elliot Quantrell had not lasted a month. No matter what transpired next week, she would not walk out. For pride's sake, she was going to have to stick it out for a while—that was—if Elliot Quantrell let her.

It was that pride which saw Kacie sailing into her office on Monday morning and, on catching sight of Elliot Quantrell, bidding him a cheerful and smiling, 'Good morning.'

Swine, she belligerently dubbed him when, as though she had something contagious, he gave her the briefest cursory glance, then promptly sealed himself off, by closing the partitioning door, and shut her out of his sight.

Kacie squashed the impulse to walk out before she

had so much as taken the cover off her typewriter. It was only by the greatest effort of remembering how she was determined to stick it out for longer than one month, that Kacie sat down at her desk at all that day.

At ten o'clock the door between the two offices opened and Kacie was summoned to dictation. Her fingers were fairly flying over her shorthand pad when, after a light tap on the woodwork, a tanned fair-haired man entered the chairman's office.

'Thought I'd better show my face,' the man addressed her employer, and Elliot broke off his rapid dictation to shake hands with him.

Kacie took this opportunity to ease her right hand, then found the newcomer had turned to observe her. She saw his smile suddenly widen, and heard delight in his every word when he exclaimed:

'Well—aren't *you* an improvement to Elliot's office!'

A hasty glance to her employer showed that he was wearing the tight-lipped look she had grown familiar with. When he made no attempt whatsoever to introduce her, the new arrival, who appeared to wear a permanent smile, apparently saw no reason why he should not find out more for himself.

'Elliot obviously isn't going to do the honours,' he said, paying no heed to the fact he had interrupted Elliot's dictation and stepping forward to take hold of her right hand. 'I'm Jonathan Davy, director *extraordinaire*, who would have returned from holiday much sooner had I known our chairman intended to break with what we all thought was unbreakable tradition and take on a female secretary.'

Kacie smiled, she couldn't help it. Jonathan Davy, whatever else he was, was clearly an outrageous flirt, but since he was so open with it, she thought him quite harmless.

'Kacie Peters,' she murmured, and seeing no reason

not to, she would have trotted out more polite social niceties, but she never got the chance.

Plainly of the opinion enough time had been wasted, Elliot Quantrell, his voice no more civil than usual, even to one of his directors, sharply cut in, 'When you've quite finished with the hand holding, Miss Peters can get on with more shorthand.'

'Still the same slave-driver?' Jonathan grinned unabashed. But he did not stay longer than to add, 'I'll see you later, Elliot. And you, Kacie, much more often, I hope,' he concluded with a smiling look to her.

Kacie expected to be hard at it with her pencil well before she heard the outer door close. But, when Elliot did not immediately take up from where he had left off, she looked up.

His eyes, she saw, were not on the matter in front of him, but on her. Quickly she realised he must be waiting for her to read back the last piece of dictation, but before she had time to refer to her notepad, he again set her adrenalin pumping, when he snarled offensively, 'Do you see it your appointed role in life to give the "come-on" to every man you meet?'

Only by the skin of her teeth did she hold back on the impulse to throw her note book at him and walk out. But a moment or two later, she had controlled her emotions, and even managed to find a modicum of surface politeness when she replied, 'Occasionally, it's been my misfortune to meet a man I would much prefer to tell where he can go, rather than suggest he should "come-on".'

Almost, although she couldn't be certain, she thought she saw movement at the corner of his mouth to suggest that her thinly veiled pointed answer had amused him. But she knew that for the most idiotic notion she'd had yet, when he tersely told her, 'I'm

not paying you to flirt on my time.' Needing no
reminder of where they had got to, he slammed
straight away into continued dictation.

The week which followed saw Kacie growing more
and more familiar with the way Elliot Quantrell
worked. There was no let up in his curt manner with
her, however, and even Jonathan Davy came in for
some of his spleen when he visited her office once too
often. Though what was said when Elliot, wearing his
usual tight-lipped expression came to his door to
observe one of his directors lingering by her desk, she
did not know. After Elliot's repressive, 'When you've
a moment, Jonathan . . .' the fair-haired man had
followed him into his office and had closed the door.
He had not appeared in her office again without some
genuine cast iron reason.

Mike Carey was still trying to date her, but he was
no problem. Cecil Glover though, was another kettle
of fish. It was seldom that he came to her office, but it
seemed to her she could never leave it without finding
him lurking around some corner. She hated the feel of
his podgy hands on her, yet time and again he would
waylay her, to touch her arm or her shoulder in what
appeared a fatherly way, but which the look in his eyes
belied. Because of his senior years and position,
instead of giving in to the urge to tell him to keep his
hands to himself, she would take a step out of his
reach and go on her way. He was soon forgotten the
moment she returned to her desk, for with so much
else to keep her busy, there was no room to think of
anything except her duties.

With work flowing in on a steady torrent, it was not
until Kacie was driving home on Friday, that it suddenly
struck her that although she was sure she had slaved
every bit as hard this week as she had the week before;
somehow, her work load had seemed easier.

Perhaps it is just that I'm getting used to Elliot Quantrell's way of working, she mused. But although not one word of praise had come from him for anything she had accomplished, nor would it she was certain, she could not deny a feeling of elation at the thought that she could cope!

That she still had energy to spare to go to the badminton club and whack the daylights out of a shuttlecock, proved it. Kacie went to bed that night, exhilarated by a sense of achievement. Give her another couple of weeks and, if not exactly able to do her job standing on her head, there wouldn't be a thing Elliot Quantrell could throw at her which she couldn't take in her stride.

'Good morning,' she chirruped brightly when she went into the office on Monday. She sat down at her desk smiling at the thought that things were improving. Elliot Quantrell had not been able to bring himself to answer her greeting, but that had definitely been a nod of acknowledgement, before he had closed his door.

Any premature idea her employer might have a human streak, was to be hit soundly on the head not half an hour later. Kacie sat in his office, her ears sharp so as not to miss a word of his instruction, when suddenly the phone rang. No doubt thinking it farcical to send her scurrying back to her desk to answer it, he indicated she should take the call on his phone.

With her pencil poised to jot down any note, she picked up the phone and said her usual, 'Mr Quantrell's secretary.'

It was not, however, a business call, and her pleasure at hearing Vincent's voice made her lose her efficient-sounding front. As a smile broke from her she forgot, for a moment, that she was not in her own office.

'Vincent!' she exclaimed. 'How are you?' She became aware of her employer's eyes on her, and on her mouth.

'Could be better,' Vincent replied. 'I thought it about time I rang to ask how the new job goes.'

'Fine,' she said, feeling constrained and wishing she had scooted to her desk to take the call, 'just fine.'

'You're getting on all right with your new boss?' he asked.

'Like a house on fire,' she lied. At one and the same time she wanted to end the call, and yet not to end it in case she hurt Vincent's feelings. Above all she wanted to change the subject. 'How's your new secretary?' she asked.

'She has a lot to learn,' he glumly replied. Then, still in that same glum tone, 'Julie's left me,' he told her flatly.

'Oh, Vincent, I'm so sorry,' she sympathised, and would have added a bracing 'I'm sure she'll come back to you' had she not spied Elliot Quantrell frowning darkly at her.

Vincent didn't wait for her to add anything, but went on, 'I need to talk to someone, Kacie. I don't suppose you'd meet me tonight for a drink somewhere, would you?'

Almost, she weakened. Almost, she forgot the terrible wrench it had been to cut Vincent out of her life. Almost she gave in to start the whole exercise once more. But then her employer gave an irritated movement, as if to say that he had more to do with his time than to sit listening to her wittering on.

Pulled two ways, Kacie was forced to tell Vincent another lie.

'Actually, I've already made arrangements for tonight which I really can't get out of.' And, hot on the heels of that, she continued, 'I must dash, someone wants me.'

Kacie strove to recapture her efficient front the moment she put the phone down. But Vincent was dear to her, and in trouble, and she had the awful feeling that, when he had needed her, she had let him down. She flicked a glance to Elliot Quantrell to let him know she was ready to resume. There was no mistaking the aggression in his face.

She was startled still when, instead of straight away making up the minutes lost, he ignored the task in hand and grated, 'So married men, too, are included on your scalp belt?'

Her eyes widened, but she was too taken aback by his verbal attack to say anything for a second. Then she recalled how on his first day back he had pulled no punches when warning her of the consequences should she dare to go after him.

Quickly she gathered her composure, and innocently replied, 'I can't help it if I find married men more agreeable than bachelors.'

Her comment drew forth not the smallest show of having amused him this time. Nor was he in the mood to dress up any of his comments in a cloak of innocence. Indeed Elliot Quantrell was at his forthright best, when he challenged, 'Why, exactly, *did* you leave Vincent Jenner's employ?'

Shaken to hear that the chairman of Quantrell Industries still did not believe her 'advancement' excuse, Kacie saw she would be wasting her time to trot out the same story again. But, since pride still demanded it was the only explanation he was going to get, she was left floundering, and came back with a reply that was no answer at all.

'Anything other than the reason I've given you, comes under the heading of "confidential".' When he looked ready to bite her head off, she reminded him, 'You'd hardly like it, if I left your employ and then blabbed any of what comes under a "confidential" label here.'

'There's no "*if*" about it,' rapidly stung her ears.

The subject closed, he began such a brisk flow of dictation that she had no time to think. It wasn't until she was back at her desk that she had a free second in which to wonder whether his final retort had meant that there was no '*if*' about her leaving his employ, or that he would not like it if she went blabbing his confidential business. It did not take long to realise she could quite rightly take it to mean both. Though when the axe would fall on her job, was anybody's guess.

Her injured pride made her feel like packing in her job before he could tell her that her services were no longer required. But then she remembered how she had determined to stick this job out for as long as she could.

Kacie stuck to her decision, but she could not help smarting whenever she thought of how, even though she worked her fingers to the bone for him, Elliot Quantrell was planning to dismiss her at the first moment to suit his convenience.

Which was why she was in no mood to be placatory when, on Thursday, he took exception to her taking personal calls at work.

The badminton tournament was over a week away, but Simon Fletcher had already started to panic about it, and rang to reassure himself that she would be at the club that night to practise.

'I promise you, Simon,' she told him, 'wild horses wouldn't keep me from joining you tonight.'

She had just put the phone down when, from his office, Elliot Quantrell barked, 'Haven't you got a phone at home?'

In Kacie's view, she had put up with his churlish

manner for long enough, and anger rose in her as she glanced through the open doorway to meet his dour look.

'I'll make a point of seeing my scalped friends, single and married, have my home number,' she bristled, but derived small satisfaction to hear his grunt of disgust before the communicating door crashed to.

Later she wondered if, in some perverse way, she had been asking him to dismiss her, the sooner to know where she stood. But Friday saw her driving home without hearing the words of dismissal she had expected. For a little while longer, she still had a job.

Her weekend followed a pattern similar to the previous one. She intended to tell Simon it might be better if he used her home phone number in future, but he was in such a state as he darted here and there seeing to travel arrangements and making sure everyone knew where the venue was, that she decided to leave it.

There was every likelihood she wouldn't be working for Quantrell Industries for much longer anyway. In any event, since she would be seeing Simon a couple of times before they set off on Friday night, she thought it most improbable he would need to phone her again.

That assumption was proved wrong. She had barely settled herself in Elliot Quantrell's office on Monday— with no cheery greeting for him that morning—when he answered the phone then, his face unsmiling as ever, passed it over to her.

If it was Vincent she just did not have the time to stay sympathising with him. Her spirits lifted only slightly to hear Simon in a lather because Angus had just rung him to say his car was in dock and might not be ready to take some of the team on Friday.

'No problem,' she quickly eased his fears. 'We can use mine.'

'I was hoping you'd say that,' said Simon, sounding much relieved. 'My Mini will only take four, and there'll be five of us. You're sure . . .' Ever the worrier, he would have gone on.

'Of course,' she speedily reassured him, the baleful look from her employer enough to tell her that he was getting not a little browned off with the interruptions he had to suffer while she arranged her private life.

'You'll be at the club tomorrow?' Simon just had to ask before she could get rid of him.

'I'll see you at half-past seven,' Kacie replied. 'Goodbye Simon,' she said firmly, and put down the phone.

Kacie took up her shorthand pad once more, and then as she felt Elliot Quantrell's hard grey eyes on her, she looked up, and unexpectedly, her heart started to pound. Suddenly, she knew, that this was it!

That second personal call from Simon had been the last straw. Any minute now, she knew she would be receiving her marching orders. Elliot tossed the pen in his hand down on to his desk, and could not hide his satisfaction when, almost pleasantly, he began to speak.

'You'll forgive me for overhearing your side of the conversation, I'm sure.' His sarcasm, however pleasantly he might choose to deliver it, she just did not need. 'Just as I'm sure,' he went on, 'you won't forgive me for saying that you'll have to cancel your date tonight.'

If he was dispensing with her services, he was going a funny way about it.

'Cancel my d . . .'

'You've seen our workload,' he reminded her, and even produced a smile. 'I'm afraid, Miss Peters, you'll be working overtime tonight.'

Why she should feel relief that he had not told her

to be on her way, Kacie did not know. But suddenly, jolted out of her preconceived notion that she would soon be jobless, she found that she too, was smiling.

'There's no need for me to cancel anything, Mr Quantrell,' she told him, her smile drawing his eyes to her mouth. 'My—er—date with Simon, isn't until tomorrow.' My, how swiftly his mood can change, Kacie thought.

One moment he was leaning back in his chair apparently in no hurry to get down to work—and the next, he was scanning the matter in front of him and, his pleasant manner gone, was terminating the brief respite with a bluntly sarcastic, 'The way my phone rings, I thought you *never* had a night off.'

Despite the bad start to the week, on Friday Kacie looked back on all she had accomplished and could not help but feel a sense of achievement. Her work came much more easily to her now, and several times yesterday, she had been able to anticipate Elliot Quantrell's requirements.

Around three that afternoon she found herself thinking of how she had to dash home, have a quick snack, and get herself and her gear round to the badminton club to pick up her passengers. It seemed to confirm that she could not be doing too badly. She had been too hard at it on other Fridays to have time for thoughts of anything unconnected with business.

Just as though thinking of him had conjured him up, Simon rang. Forgetful of the open communicating door and the fact that she had an employer whose ears never missed a thing, Kacie laughed lightly as she told Simon, 'Talk of the devil, I was just thinking about you!'

'Yes, well . . .' mumbled Simon, who had his mind set on serious matters. 'Angus has got his car back, so I thought I'd ring to tell you we won't be needing yours.'

'Oh good,' she murmured, 'I'll see you later then.'
With a friendly, 'I've got my bag packed ready,' she
prepared to say goodbye. But Simon had heard from
the organisers at the other end that, win or lose, there
was a party arranged for afterwards, and suggested it
might be better if they could stay over an extra night.

'I've rung round all the others, and they're looking
forward to it,' he enthused. 'But if it presents any
difficulty . . .'

'That means two nights away,' Kacie thought out
loud. Still, she had nothing to press her into coming
back before the others. 'That's fine by me, Simon,'
she told him. 'We can take the return journey to
London at a more leisurely pace if we come back on
Sunday.'

'Great,' said Simon, and with the air of a man with a
thousand and one things to do, he rang off, and Kacie
buried her head in her work.

At five o'clock she put the cover over her typewriter
with her thoughts again on how she must hurry home
and do all she had to before she left her flat for the
weekend.

What she did not need was Elliot Quantrell to come
out of his office and delay her. Anything else he
wanted could not be so important that it could not
wait until Monday, so she effected a 'Good night Mr
Quantrell,' and had reached the door when he
interrupted her, 'I'll see you on——'

'Tomorrow.'

'Tomorrow?' she queried, her mouth picking up at
the corners. 'Tomorrow's Saturday,' she reminded
him.

For the second time since she had known him, Elliot
Quantrell favoured her with a smile. 'True,' he replied
evenly.

'But—I don't work Saturdays',' she said slowly—

and wished she had not when all semblance of a smile abruptly left his face. In the next second he was ripping into her.

'Had I wanted a nine to five, Monday to Friday secretary, I'd have asked personnel to find me one.' Kacie bridled at his tone, but before she could get a word in edgeways, he was blistering on. 'You've known since Wednesday that I intended to take a look at that design engineer's invention up in Paisley. Surely to God,' he barked, 'you didn't think I was going to go all that way without taking along someone competent to take down notes?'

'But—you said nothing about when you were going!' Kacie protested, angry in spite of the fact that he had actually deigned to call her competent! 'Had I received advance notice, I would willingly have changed my plans and accompanied you. But, to drop it on me when I'm half way out . . .' She saw he looked ready to jump down her throat so, Kacie changed tack to quietly tell him, 'I've made arrangements to go away for the weekend. Arrangements which . . .'

'Which you'll have to cancel.' He chopped her off before she could explain a word about the badminton tournament.

'But I can't do that,' she protested, even as she protested aware she was just asking to be dismissed on the spot.

His expression tough, Elliot Quantrell ignored her stubborn look, then warned her harshly, 'Don't—push it.'

'I'm not!' she argued. 'It's just that . . .' The steely look in his grey eyes stopped her from going any further. She knew then that he was not interested in hearing her argument.

She drew on all her reserves, ready to be able to reply she did not want his beastly job anyway.

But Elliot completely shattered her hard-won composure when, with no easing in his tough expression, he told her, 'Look—since you've done your job these past weeks without the female wiles coming into it, I've begun to accept you as your male counterpart. But if you can't drop whatever you have planned—as in the interest of his career any male secretary worth his salt would—then as far as I'm concerned, I've got myself the wrong secretary.'

Kacie swallowed, and hovered half-way between being Scotland bound tomorrow, and being unemployed. If she went to Scotland with him, she could come back and still not know where she stood.

'Are you saying,' she asked slowly, 'that if I don't accompany you to Scotland tomorrow—there's no point in my coming in on Monday?'

'Your intelligence has obviously not deserted you,' he replied coolly, pinning her with his hard grey look.

'Then might I know,' said Kacie, trying to appear as cool as him, 'if it's your intention to dismiss me at the first convenient moment—on our return?'

To her mind, she still had not agreed to accompany him. But from the small movement at the corners of his mouth, she had a feeling he had sensed victory.

That faint suggestion of a smile had gone when, his tone smooth, he unbent sufficiently to inform her, 'Your work so far, has been satisfactory.' But while her spirits perked up to hear him admit that much, all he would add, was a cool, 'Whatever else I may be, Miss Peters, I hope you believe I'm a fair man.'

Kacie was aware then, that in her quest to know if her employment with him was permanent, he had gone as far as he would. But, thinking back over his business dealings, she knew at first hand that they did not come straighter than him.

She found herself reluctantly asking, 'Where do I meet you tomorrow?'

She knew there was no one more sure of himself than Elliot Quantrell when, without so much as a batted eyelid, he smartly returned, 'I'll call for you—eight-thirty sharp.'

'I live in . . .'

'I know where you live,' he replied, to let her know he had been through her personnel file with a fine tooth comb. Kacie moved and was going through the door to the corridor when he called after her, 'You've an overnight bag packed—bring it.'

Without turning, and without saying another word, she continued on her way.

CHAPTER THREE

SATURDAY dawned cold and cheerless. Kacie got out of bed in matching mood. Never had it occurred to her when she had heard how Elliot Quantrell was forever here, there and everywhere; that she would be too!

She still felt the guilt which had entered her when, faced with the option of Simon Fletcher never speaking to her again, or starting to look for another job, she had picked up the phone to cancel the arrangements with her badminton partner.

Simon's incredulous, 'You can't *mean* it!' still rang in her ears. As did his reminder that she had said nothing about having to work on Saturday when he had spoken with her only a few hours before.

'I didn't know then,' she had told him awkwardly. She could not recall where in last Wednesday's conversation Elliot Quantrell had said he intended to view the design engineer's invention on Saturday. 'That is,' she amended, 'I must have known my boss had work on out of the area tomorrow—it just never occurred to me he would want me along.'

Apart from where it affected the tournament, Simon had no interest whatsoever in what went on in her office. 'I call it a damned poor show,' he said and put down the phone.

Accepting that it was unlikely they would get to Paisley and back in one day, she took her sports gear out of her bag and repacked it. The prospect of being incarcerated with her taciturn employer for hours on end, was not a pleasing one.

At twenty-past eight, Kacie was dressed with ten

38

minutes to spare before Elliot Quantrell would call for
her. She recalled his parting command for her to bring
her overnight bag and felt mutiny stir within her. If he
had known that, then he must have had an ear to her
conversation when Simon had phoned; and must have
known for going on *two hours* that she had a non-
working weekend planned!

That Elliot Quantrell had left it until five o'clock to
tell her to cancel her alternative weekend arrangements
made her anger complete. Then her flat bell rang. She
choked down rebellion. He was her employer. She
picked up her bag, and went to join him.

Any civil pleasantry she might have found for the tall,
sheepskin coat clad man on the doorstep, was made
irrelevant. She discovered, when he relieved her of her
overnight bag with more of a grunt than a greeting, that
he too had got out of bed on the wrong side.

His car was up to the minute, speedy, and efficient.
In next to no time her bag was stowed, she was
ensconced in the passenger seat, and they were away.

As they sped down the motorway she was still
thinking of the morose company she was committed to
spend the rest of the day with. She was aware of
Elliot's capacity for intense concentration, but as the
car effortlessly ate up the miles, she was determined
not to speak until she was spoken to.

Kacie left him to concentrate on the road in front.
Very little had been said by the time he pulled into a
service area and told her they would stop for a ten
minute coffee break.

The world and his wife appeared to be travelling
that day, she observed when she preceded Elliot
Quantrell into the crowded self-service café.

'Find a couple of seats,' he instructed her briefly.
Having thus issued his orders, he left her to find the
impossible, while he went to join the coffee queue.

Visions of his displeasure at their having to drink their
coffee standing up, had Kacie going up and down the
aisles in her search. She had just spotted Elliot bearing
down on her, and had decided they were just going to
jolly well have to stand, when someone touched her arm.

'You can have my seat, love,' said a young man with
a football favour on his lapel. 'We're just leaving.'

Her smile warm, she gave him her grateful thanks,
and the young man pulled his football supporter
friend out into the aisle. Kacie slid along the vacated
bench, but as she looked up, she saw the young man
was disposed to linger for a chat.

'Are you going far?' he asked, but when Elliot
arrived to glower from one to the other, he did not
wait for an answer. With a, 'Have a safe journey,' he
took himself and his companion off.

With a veritable hub-bub of conversations going on
around her, Kacie downed her coffee in silence.
Today's visit had been dropped on her without giving
her chance to check her notes but the very fact she
would have to raise her voice above the clatter if she
made any enquiry, decided her against doing so. For
all she knew, the matter could be highly confidential.
Elliot Quantrell was enough of a bear with a sore head
without her inviting the full blast of his aggression.

She saw his cup go down and, anticipating his
move, she was already reaching for her shoulder bag
when, curtly, he asked, 'Ready?'

She supposed she must be grateful that he had
bothered to enquire. The way he was behaving today,
it wouldn't have surprised her had he just walked off
and left her to follow.

She received more unexpected courtesy when, at the
car, he shrugged out of his sheepskin and suggested
she might feel the benefit later, if she disposed of the
full length coat she had on over her dress.

'Thank you,' she murmured, but with the temperature feeling colder the further north they went, and with her coat lying alongside his in the back seat, she was glad to get inside the car again and feel the warmth from the heater.

Instead of the well cut business suit he usually wore, Elliot was now clad in the more casual sweater and slacks. When they had been on the road again for another twenty minutes, Kacie found her thoughts had wandered. She was actually contemplating how, without a jacket, his shoulders were as broad as ever. She was quick to turn her mind deliberately away from such personal matters.

'This Mr Atkins we're going to see . . .' She broke the silence with the only non-personal matter she could think of for the moment.

'Aitken,' he corrected her. 'His name is Dougal Aitken.'

'I didn't have time to check the file,' she reminded him, and wished her memory was as elephantine as his. With so much happening daily in the office, she still did not see how she could be expected to remember the name of everyone they dealt with. She then concentrated on what he was saying when Elliot, in the same civil tones in which he had asked would she like to remove her coat, went on to refresh her memory and to fill in the blanks.

'Mr Aitkin doesn't belong to any one particular firm then?' she questioned. 'I thought that Quantrell Industries only dealt with major companies.'

'In the main, we do,' he stated. 'But while I've never bought an invention from Dougal yet, some of his futuristic crackpot ideas have been so near coming off that it can only be a matter of time before he comes up with an idea which is commercially viable.'

'You've taken—a—personal interest in him?' Kacie,

guessing she was sticking her neck out, dared to ask. For, as far as she could see, there could be no other reason why the chairman of the big conglomerate should give up his weekend when he had any number of highly qualified men at his disposal whom he could have sent in his stead.

'You, Miss Peters,' he drawled after a moment, 'are as smart, as you are efficient.' Which left her to wonder if she had just been handed a compliment, or the reverse. It had been a compliment, she thought, when he went on, 'Dougal Aitken has been a personal friend of mine since the days when he was my lecturer at university.'

Before she could start to glow that he thought her smart *and* efficient, Elliot proceeded to leave her in no doubt that there was no place for friendship in business.

'While I'm gratified that he still remembers my quirk for wanting to know how everything works, and always approaches me first with anything new, Dougal appreciates that, first and foremost, I'm a businessman. Which means,' he told her in case she had not been smart enough to work it out for herself, 'that unless he can prove his machine will make money for both him and my company, then I won't be interested.'

Which statement had Kacie realising that, hard though Elliot Quantrell had made himself sound, he must have some affection for his former tutor. Why else would he put himself out, when he could have sent just about anybody all this way? Qualifying that though, was the memory of how, within a very short space of her meeting him, he had laid it on the line that he never mixed business with pleasure.

Little else had been said by either of them when, around one o'clock, he pulled off the motorway, and advised her they would stop for lunch. He drove to a private hotel off the beaten track.

The morning which had started with both of them in a grumpy state, had been lightened by their brief conversation, and when Elliot escorted her to a table, his more amiable mood had rubbed off on to her.

'What would you like to drink?' he deigned to ask, when she had thought they would launch straight into the soup, and subsequent courses, and then leave again.

'A sherry, if we have time,' she replied politely, and was on her best behaviour—as he appeared to be—when her sherry and his Scotch were brought to the table, and he further deigned to consult her over what she would like to eat.

Kacie even found herself offering him a smile when, after the soup arrived, they both reached for the pepper-mill at the same time.

'After you,' he gallantly backed off, his eyes coming away from her curved mouth to look into her eyes.

Unaccountably Kacie experienced the most peculiar fluttery feeling in her heart, and she lowered her eyes to find she was having to concentrate really hard on the most simple procedure of grinding some pepper into her soup.

A delicious home-made steak and kidney pie soon had her realising that the fluttery sensation must have been some kind of hunger pangs. She tucked in with a will, which brought forth the unexpected personal comment:

'You—hm—don't have to diet?'

'I'm too energetic for fat to have a chance,' she replied. About to explain how she played badminton two or three times a week, and sometimes more, she looked across to him, only to be taken aback to note all sign of civility gone! Why he should be looking so darkly at her, she had no clue.

'I can believe that,' he muttered sourly. 'I assume you made contact with your lover before . . .'

'Lover!' she exclaimed, too shaken to be able to hop on to his wavelength.

'While I appreciate you have more than one,' his sarcasm in full flow, he ignored her wide eyed surprise, 'surely it goes beyond the bounds of etiquette, not to advise the man you intended to spend the weekend with, that the weekend is off?'

'Simon!' she exclaimed. 'You mean Simon!' Rapidly she understood the implication. As anger flared into life, she was in two minds whether to leave Elliot Quantrell to think what the devil he liked, or whether to put him right.

'He's the one who phones you most frequently.'

'Well he won't be phoning me again,' she retorted, her turn to be sour.

'Took it badly, did he?' Elliot jibed.

'He wasn't—well pleased,' said Kacie stiffly. It took all her stubborn will not to mention the word badminton, much less the fact that should she ever dare show her face at the club again, Simon would probably cut her dead.

'You told him you were coming away with me instead,' Elliot queried, his sarcastic tone gone and, it seemed, his aggression with it.

Quickly Kacie recovered from being shaken at what he had thought. The fact that, for all his bland front, Elliot appeared to be taking some sort of fiendish delight in the belief he had scuppered her weekend plans, put a very different complexion on the matter. She could not wait then to tell him just how wrong he was.

'I told him that my employer felt it imperative I work this weekend,' she replied. 'Simon was a little cross. But he knows deep down that Sue is every bit as good as I . . .'

'Good God!' The exclamation cut her off before she could explain further. 'You're telling me, you—swop each other around!'

'You've got it all wrong,' Kacie told him coldly. 'Simon, Sue and I, are all members of the same badminton club.' Any pleasure she might have found in showing him that he did not get it right every time, had gone. 'All I meant to convey was that since I'm unable to partner Simon in a badminton tournament this weekend, Sue Baylis will have to play in my place.'

'You were playing—this tournament—away from home?' he questioned curtly. Although his look of distaste had gone, Elliot did not seem particularly impressed by her revelation.

Kacie nodded. 'I was going to drive. Simon rang yesterday to say Angus had got his car back from the garage, so I wouldn't have to bother.'

Any reply he would have made was held back when, their main course disposed of, the waiter came to clear away their used dishes and commented he would bring the menu for them to select dessert.

After he had gone, Kacie cancelled out any idea of there being an improvement in her employer's earlier grumpy attitude.

He was all terseness and aggression, when icily he enquired, 'Is Vincent Jenner a member of this badminton club too?'

'I've had enough—to eat,' said Kacie stiffly. She had had enough of him, his manner, and his sudden penchant for seeing evil in everything she did. 'I'll hunt up the powder-room—if you'll excuse me,' she tacked on, and pushed back her chair.

She recognised certain courtesies must be inbred in him in that he rose from his chair at the moment she moved. But with her chin tilted a proud fraction higher, she felt not the least inclined to give him the briefest glance of acknowledgement. Proudly, she walked from the dining-room.

It was late afternoon when they reached their destination, and Kacie could not wait to get out of the car. For if she had taken a vow not to speak to Elliot then her companion doubly endorsed it—the silence had been deafening for the rest of the journey.

Dougal Aitken must have heard the car for he came hurrying to greet them as if from nowhere. At first the bald-headed man with a straggly white beard and moth-eaten sweater, put Kacie more in mind of a down and out than of an ex-university lecturer. In direct contrast to Elliot, he proved to be a chatter-box, and had such an infectious way with him, that Kacie felt her low spirits lighten.

'Elliot, my boy!' he boomed warmly as the two shook hands. Then he caught sight of her, 'And who's this you've brought to see me?' he asked.

'My secretary,' Elliot informed him. 'If your latest invention is as good as it sounds, Dougal, we may need her. Kacie, meet my old friend and mentor, Dougal Aitken,' he said, and finished the introduction while she recovered from the shock of hearing Elliot call her by her first name, and Dougal soundly wrung her hand.

'Florence insists that I take you straight into the house for a cup of tea, but I'm sure you'd much rather come and take a look in the workshop,' Dougal opined, so eager to have his invention inspected, it would, Kacie thought, take the hardest heart to deny him.

She wouldn't have put it past Elliot to say a cup of tea would not come amiss, so he went up a degree in her estimation when he replied, 'Lead the way.'

With her shoulder bag clutched under her arm, she trailed after the two men to an over-large shed which appeared ready to fall down if anyone so much as sneezed heavily.

The inside was brightly lit, and on first sight seemed to house nothing but a jumble of old machinery, until Dougal made tracks for his latest pride and joy. Kacie was all poised to get out her notepad to take down the notes, but she was ignored while Dougal and Elliot pored over some intricate looking drawings.

Ten minutes later she heartily wished she had foreseen she would be left to stand about on a concrete floor in an unheated outhouse. She might then have thought to grab her coat from the car.

Forgotten by the two engineers who conversed in incomprehensible language, she steadily grew colder and colder. The drawings were put aside while oddly shaped pieces of metal were turned downside up, and pumped this way and that. Kacie began to wonder how her iced up fingers were going to hold a pencil when note taking time came; let alone how she would get them to write.

It amazed her that neither man—Elliot's sheepskin was in the car too—was aware of the below freezing temperature. But another glance to where the two where now engrossed in what looked like a dismantling of the project, was to tell her she could fall over in a backward stiff line, and they would still be too involved to hear the crash.

But the invention was so important to Dougal, and with his work being so thoroughly and seriously investigated by Elliot, she knew that neither would thank her if she interrupted them to mention her chattering teeth.

There was a sudden interruption. It came from a blond haired man in his late twenties, who entered the workshop, and began,

'Mother said . . .' He stopped dead when he caught sight of Kacie. 'Whatever it was Mother said, I've

forgotten,' he said, and came over to her with his
father's grin splitting his face, so he had no need to
add, 'I'm Gavin Aitken, non-engineering son of
Dougal.'

'Kacie Peters,' she introduced herself, and as his
manner was as infectious as Dougal's, she just had to
add, 'non-engineering secretary of Elliot.'

Gavin laughed, and as they shook hands, Kacie
could not help but emit a sound of amusement.
Abruptly her smile faded when—his concentration
broken, she guessed, at hearing her take it upon
herself to use his first name—Elliot turned to glare at
her, then promptly turned his attention back to the
invention.

'You're freezing!' Gavin exclaimed, reminding her
he was still holding her hand. 'Come over to the
house, do,' he urged, and would have pulled her from
the workshop, had she not refused to budge.

'I'm here to take notes,' she told him firmly, and
gave a flicked glance to where her employer now
appeared to be putting the invention back together
again.

'Then have my coat,' Gavin insisted, and whipped
off his tweed jacket and wrapped it around her
shoulders before she had chance to decline.

She had started to feel marginally warmer when
finally the two men finished at the workbench, but the
glacial look Elliot served her when he observed her
standing with Gavin and draped in Gavin's over-large
jacket, was enough to turn her spine into an icicle.

So far, she hadn't been called upon to take one
solitary note. But she knew from Dougal's bright eyed
expression and his grin which would put a Cheshire
Cat's to shame, that the performance of his invention
had come up to scratch.

'We'll talk contract details over that cup of tea

Florence promised,' Elliot told Dougal, looking
through Kacie.

The two men walked in front of her and Gavin as
they left the workshop and went towards the house.
When Gavin held the sitting-room door open for her
to go through, Kacie saw Dougal had not wasted a
second to tell his wife the news that Elliot was going to
take his invention. They were hugging each other, and
so obviously cock-a-hoop that Dougal's long, hard and
detailed work had at last paid off, that Kacie did not
like to go forward to intrude on this hard-earned
moment.

But with Gavin waiting to come forward, she
stepped into the room, and glanced to the roaring fire
that blazed a welcome.

'Break it up you two,' quipped Gavin, and went to
shake hands with Elliot, which left Kacie to think he
had assumed Elliot too involved with the invention
previously to observe the formalities.

She was then introduced to Florence Aitken, who
did no more than shake her hand before she too
exclaimed, 'You're frozen!' adding 'Come away to the
fire.' While Dougal suggested that this called for
champagne, his wife cast a resigned look at his
sweater, and with the air of someone who had given up
trying to keep him tidy, she bustled out to make a pot
of tea.

Kacie came into her own when Dougal's contract
with Quantrell Industries was discussed. Life had
come back to her fingers sitting next to the fire and
her pencil flew over her note pad.

For all Elliot had made himself sound a hard-
headed business man, Kacie could not help noticing
how straight he was in all his dealings. Dougal was so
over the moon he would have agreed to any terms, and
was wide open to being short changed. But frequently

Elliot would stop and refer to some finer detail which
Dougal had missed. The end result was an agreement
which treated Dougal handsomely. Even then Elliot
insisted that when the contract came through Dougal
should sign nothing before he had taken it to his
solicitor.

Excitement was still in the air when Kacie put her
note pad away, and more tea and fruit cake was served.
When Gavin, with his eyes on her, suggested they
should all go out to dinner that night to celebrate,
Elliot surprised her by cutting in to say, 'Can't be
done, I'm afraid. We have to be on our way shortly.'

'You're going back to London—tonight!' Gavin
exclaimed. 'You've driven hundreds of miles! You
won't get back before . . .'

'Elliot's a busy man, son,' Dougal chipped in,
looking at his former student. 'You were always off
somewhere in a hurry in the old days, Elliot,' he
recalled.

Kacie was still wondering why on earth she had
brought an overnight bag if she would be sleeping in
her own bed that night—or rather morning, since she
couldn't see how they could possibly arrive back in
London before the early hours—when Elliot said they
must be on their way.

All three Aitkens came to see them off. After
goodbyes had been said and Florence and Dougal
stepped back from the car, Gavin came over to Kacie's
window.

Elliot was impatient to be off. But the Aitkens were
such a nice family, and it just wasn't in Kacie's nature
to be churlish. Regardless of the cold, she pressed the
switch to slide down the window.

'I've just remembered that I've been invited to a
wedding in London next weekend,' said Gavin with
his usual smile. Kacie smiled back and pretended she

had not noticed the impatient movement from the driver's side of the car. 'Would you mind if I looked you up while I'm there?'

With her employer champing at the bit to be away, Kacie saw only one quick way to end this conversation. 'I'd like that,' she said, but had no time in which to give Gavin her phone number, because the car had started up, and they were off.

Kacie pressed the switch to close the window. It had not taken long for Elliot to change back from the pleasantly civil person he had been in Florence and Dougal Aitken's company. She thought she heard him mutter some disbelieving comment about Gavin's sudden memory of a wedding he had to attend in London.

But there was nothing wrong with her hearing when he suddenly blasted: 'You can't resist it, can you?'

Dumbfounded she turned in her seat and had her ears further assaulted. 'First the encouraging smile, then the come-hither look. Married or single,' he snarled, 'no man's safe from you!'

Shock at his unwarranted attack kept her silent for all of a second. Then, she cared not a button that he was her employer, and lost no more time in letting him know.

'You are!'

'My stars!' he exploded. 'I hope to God you don't think *I'm* in contention!'

There was no civil answer to that. For the next hour Kacie silently seethed from his offensive remarks. There was not a name bad enough for him in her vocabulary as the car sped towards London.

It infuriated her that while she lived by the tenet that a friendly smile here and there hurt no one, the tyrant of a man by her side should see such normal friendliness only as a sign of encouragement to the opposite sex. To hear him say as much, she fumed as on they drove, showed that he thought she displayed an idiotic grin any time some male in trousers came anywhere near!

She was still fuming when he halted the car outside a country hotel. She was in two minds whether to tell him she did not want dinner, and would stay in the car while he ate. But just the mere thought of a meal made her realise she was ravenously hungry.

Without a smile, she got out of the car. When she observed him extract both his overnight bag and hers from the boot, she quickly saw that they would be staying at the hotel that night rather than driving back to London.

Wordlessly she went with him into the hotel, and stood silently by while he took it upon himself to sign both of them in. They were being shown up to their rooms when she recalled that her autocratic boss had never said they would be driving back to London that night. In answer to Gavin's celebratory dinner suggestion, he had merely said, 'We have to be on our way', she remembered.

She was shown to a room next door to his. Even if she had wanted to say anything to him, she did not get the chance. With a curt, 'I'll see you in ten minutes,' he stepped into his room and from her sight.

Kacie entered her room, the translation clear. Elliot Quantrell wanted his dinner and would not excuse any feminine lateness should he have to wait one minute longer than necessary.

Precisely ten minutes after his curt utterance, she stepped from her room to meet her employer as he came from his. Wordlessly, with not so much as the smallest curve to touch her mouth, she fell into step with him. Even if she had to bolt her food, this was going to be the shortest dinner on record.

In the event, the good manners instilled in her since childhood, made her unable to attack her plate like some half starved animal. As she disposed of her first course and started on her second, Elliot Quantrell appeared to have nothing he wanted to say to her. And she felt just the same.

She imagined that dinner would be concluded without conversation. But suddenly her employer broke the silence to ask pointedly, 'Do you always sulk, when taken to task?'

'Sulk!' The exclaimed word left her despite her determination not to let him needle her again. 'I'm not sulking,' she said hotly.

'Then—where's the famous smile?'

Kacie had never before thought of hitting a man. But she was so angry then that not only did she want to physically lash out at him, but she came within a hair's breadth of doing so. Control of her temper arrived in the nick of time.

My God, she thought, with visions of her losing her job if she had let fly in the semi-populated hotel restaurant. What had come over her! She wondered if she was cracking up!

'Far be it from me, Mr Quantrell, to smile, or to send any facial expression your way,' she said stiffly, 'which might be construed in any way as being coy.'

Her flicked glance showed he was frowning at her reminder of his stated intention to dismiss her if she so much as sent him one coy glance. She was fairly certain he would either endorse that stated intent, or say something of an equally unpalatable nature, but he surprised her by doing neither.

'What happened to—Elliot?'

For another brief moment, she had the weirdest idea he was inviting her to use his first name. Common sense told her he was doing nothing of the kind. She

remembered how she had told Gavin she was the
'non-engineering secretary of Elliot' and knew then
that he was either needling her for the pure hell of it,
or he was again taking her to task—this time, for her
impudent free use of his name.

She was tempted to risk instant dismissal by telling
him exactly what she would like to happen to Elliot.
But even as she bit down the impulse, a stubbornness
awoke in her that compelled her not to apologise. He
should have been too occupied to have overheard
anyway.

Plainly he was waiting for her to reply. 'It was a
joke,' she murmured, and when from his frown she
saw that did not suit either, she gave up. 'I've gone
off—desserts,' she told him, and fed up, angry, and
finding him the most confusing of men, she smartly
left the table, and the restaurant.

On her hurried way to her room she reassessed her
use of the word confusing. Elliot Quantrell wasn't so
much confusing, but totally infuriating, she decided,
and charged round the corner only to go sprawling
backwards when she cannoned straight into the
handsome hotel manager coming from the opposite
direction.

It took them a moment or two to sort themselves
out. Back on her feet, Kacie found a smile to go with
her insistence that it was all her fault, but the hotel
manager was most concerned about the shock she had
received from their collision.

'Are you sure you won't have a brandy?' he pressed,
when all Kacie wanted as she observed Elliot bearing
down on them was to be on her way. The manager
had got as far as, 'If you prefer to drink in your room,
I can easily . . .' when Elliot brushed him aside and
caught hold of her arm to forcibly propel her around
the corner and along to the door of her room.

From his thunderous face Kacie could tell Elliot was furious. But she was furious too, not only at his unpardonable rudeness to a hotel manager who had only the well-being of his guests at heart, but at the high-handed way he as good as frog marched her to her room.

Control on her temper had again neared breaking point when his hand snaked out to take her door key from her. It strained to a mere thread of control when, just as though he intended to lock her in for the night, he opened the door, pushed her inside, and followed her in.

He lost no time in letting rip. 'My God! Do you never stop! Is it a disease with you or something? From football fan to hotel manager you can't keep from . . .'

Crack! The sound of her right hand landing bang on target rent the air. Her control had gone. She would not stand for anyone talking to her like that—no matter who they were.

In the suspended silence that followed while the red haze went from in front of her eyes, Kacie realised what she had just done, and felt shattered. She was as appalled by the fact she had just swiped her employer a vicious blow that had almost broken her wrist, as Elliot seemed absolutely astounded that—clearly for the first time in his life—some female had landed a blow on him.

Kacie was still trying to surface from the enormity of what she had just done, when she saw his thunderstruck expression change to one of the utmost fury. Hastily, she took a step back, but as an enraged growl left him, and he grabbed a hold of her, she knew she was going nowhere until he had evened up the score.

'You really do ask for it, lady,' he snarled. She was

certain from his fury that he was about to box her ears, but suddenly he hauled her up close. It was then she realised he had a very different punishment in mind!

She opened her mouth to shriek out a protest. It was never heard. Elliot silenced her by placing his angry mouth over hers.

Frantically she pushed and pummelled, but he would not let her go, and she found she was held more firmly when his hands left her arms, and then came about her to encircle her slender frame.

Try as she might, she could not make one scrap of headway in pushing him away. She tried to twist her head sideways, but she could not break the contact he had with her mouth. She knew then that by serving him that blow she had made him as mad as the devil. Elliot demanded retribution—he would not give up until that retribution had been taken.

Yet, while she still tried to get free, her heart pumping erratically as his mouth continued to plunder hers, she lost sight of what all this was about. She aimed an ineffectual bunched fist at his shoulder, and then found, as though someone else was moving it, that her hand had opened out.

Somehow, without any instruction from her, that hand was sliding over his shoulder, while her other hand flattened out and moved to join it across his back. All she could do then was to wonder at the feel of him, of his warmth; without knowing it, she was kissing him in return.

Held close in his arms, their mouths parted, but only briefly. Elliot claimed her mouth for a second time, and Kacie, pliant in his arms, made no resistance.

A small moan of pleasure left her. Then suddenly he abruptly pushed her from him.

It was a shock to find him gone from her arms. It

was another shock to realise that not only had he kissed her, but that she had responded! As she stood on legs that felt like jelly, and stared at him, Elliot, to her mind, looked to be fairly shaken himself.

She heard him groan.

It was that exclamation which quickly brought her round. As clear as day Kacie knew that whatever part either of them had to play in what had just taken place, she would get the blame.

'You—started it,' she accused, but her voice came out huskily, and lacked any conviction.

Elliot threw her a fierce look. 'Get yourself to bed,' he thundered, and slammed out.

Which left Kacie with hours in which to wonder not only what on earth had come over her to make her respond to the brute the way she had: but also to wonder if, come daylight, she would still have a job?

CHAPTER FOUR

PLACID! After a fitful night's sleep Kacie wondered when had she ever thought of herself as placid. Memory of the hand-stinging slap she had served Elliot Quantrell came again when, as she bathed and dressed, her right hand seemed to feel a shade tender.

She anticipated that he would want to make an early start. But, as she hurried to the restaurant, she wished she could forget all about the happenings of the previous evening.

At the breakfast table, she pondered—should she order coffee for one, or two. But when she suggested to the waiter that Mr Quantrell would join her shortly, she was informed that he had already breakfasted.

Clearly Elliot had no intentions of hanging about. Kacie saw she had better make haste if she did not want to get left behind.

'Just coffee and toast, please.' She gave her order, and tried not to feel fidgety at the thought—would Elliot leave her behind? When she remembered the fury in the blow she had dished out, she did not doubt that he would. Nor did she doubt that at the first opportunity he would tell her, in his usual blunt way, that he had no room on his staff for females who resorted to physical violence.

She recalled the fairness she had seen in him. Would he, she wondered, be fair enough to see that the kiss of retribution he had taken more than evened up the score? She grew agitated all over again, because it had not stopped at one kiss. She had wanted more. She wrenched her mind from the thought that if that slap had not earned her the sack, then the very fact she had been so responsive in his arms almost certainly had.

Steadily she munched through her toast, keeping her eyes on the glass partitioning of the restaurant in case Elliot strode by on his way out.

Then, like a bolt from the blue, she made the most startling discovery. Suddenly, without having to think about it, she knew—she wanted to keep her job! Staggered, it took all of a minute for her to take in, when she stood every chance of being dismissed, just how badly she wanted to go on working for Elliot!

The work she did for him was often complicated and kept her fully alert. But Kacie had to face the fact that never before had she ever felt the same satisfaction which came from doing a job well, and which came from working for, and with—a man such as him!

She left the restaurant without finishing her coffee. As she went she knew that she was going to fight tooth and nail to hang on to her job—even if, although that slap had been much deserved, it meant she had to apologise for what she had done.

She went straight to Elliot's room to tell him she was ready to go whenever he said. Her first sight of him showed he was as grim faced as he had been when he had left her room last night.

'Get your bag,' he instructed curtly, 'we'll go now.' This was definitely not the moment for her to get in with her apology.

Not long after, she was settled in the car, and they were off. With hours of driving in front of them she saw no need to rush to get all that stewed inside her said. Besides, he had been like a crocodile with an ache in every tooth yesterday morning too, but had mellowed a trifle towards lunch time.

Not that his mellow mood had lasted for very long. As the tyres ate up the tarmac Kacie was aware that she was going to have to choose her moment carefully.

Silently she rehearsed exactly how she was going to approach the very important matter of her continued employment. Then, unexpectedly, a shiver suddenly took her.

'Are you cold?' Elliot queried, his tone more curt than civil, but for all that, suddenly her decision to wait for the right moment departed. That he had spoken at all, seemed encouraging.

'I'm fine,' she told him. 'It's lovely and warm in here.'

She turned to look at him, and was ready with her rehearsed speech. But as she took in his stern aristocratic profile, every rehearsed word went from her. She forgot about her job, and remembered instead his slighting references to her character. All she knew then was that she did not want him to continue in the bad opinion he had formed of her.

'About last night . . .' she began, before she had given herself a chance to get sorted what it was exactly she wanted to tell him.

'Forget it,' he advised with stony repression.

'But . . .'

'I said, forget it,' he clipped. 'I'm in no mood for post mortems.'

'I didn't mean about . . .' Oh crumbs, she thought, knowing she would say it all wrong even before she started. She tried again, 'I wasn't referring to what happened after . . .' and failed miserably.

Seconds of silence elapsed. Try as she might to stay cool, her own sudden inadequacy to get said what she wanted to get said combined with his gruff inaccessibility made her lose her temper again.

'I'm merely trying to show you,' the determined part of her nature set off again, albeit her tone was not as pleasant as it had been, 'that I'm nowhere near to being the loose-living sort of female you seem to think I am.'

'It showed,' he grunted, 'when I had you in my arms.'

Her stomach did a small somersault at his reminder of how, after her initial struggle, she had not backed off, but had shown an eagerness for his kisses.

'I'm not usually like that,' she told him woodenly. 'I . . .'

'Spare me the details of what you're more "usually" like,' he gritted. 'There's nothing wrong with my imagination.' Insultingly he added, 'I have no wish, whatsoever, to hear a diatribe on the various beds you've vacated.'

'You evil minded swine! I won't have . . .'

'For God's sake shut up,' he blasted her, 'and let me concentrate on my driving.'

'Damn your driving!' she flared, beside herself with rage. 'I won't shut up.' Furiously, she charged on. 'Contrary to your opinion that I'm some sort of raving nymphomaniac who prowls about terrorising hotel managers——'

'You'd have been having one hell of a party in your room with an hotel manager had I not come along when I did,' Elliot slammed back to advise that there was nothing wrong with his ears, nor his eyesight either.

'If you'd come along a moment sooner, you'd have seen that manager picking me up off the floor after we'd cannoned into each other when we both charged round the corner at the same time,' Kacie hurled at him. 'He could see I was winded—was it so unnatural that he should think I might be in need of a brandy?'

'You had enough wind to find a smile for him, I noticed,' Elliot returned. Kacie gave up.

For the next twenty miles, her thoughts were a jumbled mixture. Why, when swine was too nice a name for him, it should have entered her soul back there to want his good opinion, she didn't know.

He could roast in hell before she would throw him a bucket of water or ever try to vindicate herself again. Since she had openly called him a swine, an evil minded one at that, she saw it a foregone conclusion that Monday would see Mr Owens in personnel looking for her *male* counterpart. She reckoned she didn't care a damn about that either.

By lunch time Kacie had simmered down. Had she nursed thoughts that Elliot might mellow as the day wore on, then the briefest stop for a sandwich, eaten in stony silence, soon showed her differently.

As London drew nearer and nearer the anger she had felt towards the silent man beside her diminished. As he turned the car into the road where she lived, she owned to feeling quite fed up, and certain that any goodbye he bade her would be in the shape of a curt, verbal dismissal from her job.

When he stopped the car outside her door and went to collect her bag from the boot, she took her bag from him, and then asked belligerently, 'Well—do I come into the office tomorrow—or don't I?'

From his lofty height, Elliot Quantrell looked down at her. Refusing to look away, Kacie felt the urge to hit him a second time when, deliberately, she felt, he chose to misunderstand her.

'You're suggesting you want a couple of days off in lieu of yesterday and today?'

'I'm suggesting nothing of the kind,' she hissed. 'I just want to know, since I've been provoked into acting like the female I am rather than the male secretary you prefer, if you—who did the provoking—intend to hold it against me.'

Without a word he turned and walked away from her, and Kacie thought that was it—she was out of a job. She moved to the pavement, her chin tilted.

With a ramrod stiff back she opened the entrance door to where she lived, and then became aware that the car had not been started up yet. Casually, her expression little short of haughty, she turned to see Elliot standing by the driver's door of his car watching her.

'Be in the office at nine sharp tomorrow, Kacie Peters,' he commanded shortly.

She turned and entered the block of flats. Elliot's car was in motion before she had closed the outer door. Her face expressionless, she climbed the stairs to her flat and inserted her key in the door.

Her face stayed woodenly immobile as she walked into her flat and placed her bag down on the floor. She closed the door, and leant against it. Then, unable to hold it in any longer, Kacie smiled.

Perhaps because her sleep had come only in snatches the previous night, she slept well that Sunday. But there was no smile to be seen on her face when she got up the next morning. She awoke with a headache, felt shivery, and knew she was coming down with a heavy cold. In the hope of killing the bug before it could develop any further, she downed a couple of aspirin, and was at the office at nine sharp.

She had not expected Elliot to notice she was one degree below par, and though she felt like death, she bade him a bright, 'Good morning.'

Later she was taking his dictation, when she realised he never missed a thing. When a tickle on her nose made her dab at it with her handkerchief, in the same breath as his dictation, so that she almost took that down too, he challenged her curtly.

'Have you got a cold?'

Sympathy yet! 'I wouldn't dare,' she replied shortly. The short aggressive interchange seemed funny and, unable to help it, her mouth quirked up at the corners. Strangely it appeared he shared the same sense of humour. There was a definite quirk to the corners of his mouth too—brief while it lasted.

He soon sobered to fire, 'Where were we?'

That Monday morning was as busy as every Monday and lunch time was upon them in no time. Kacie went out to grab a bite to eat, and free at last to think of something other than work, she decided she was feeling much better.

She re-entered the Quantrell building after her break, and was waylaid by Cecil Glover. When he enquired how she was getting on, and his 'fatherly' arm came about her shoulders, she found her tolerance to the man had been stretched once too often.

'Will you kindly keep your hands to yourself,' she suddenly erupted. She was too nauseated by his sneaky attempts to cuddle her to back down when, with angry red colour surging to his face, he shouted at her.

Kacie sighed, as with Cecil Glover's apoplectic, 'Do you know who you're talking to? I'll report you to your superior,' still ringing in her ears, she headed for the cloakroom. Whatever bug she had picked up, it must have lowered her tolerance level.

Cecil Glover had not appreciated her suggestion that he should go and find someone who might welcome his pathetic overtures. Kacie knew that for fact when she saw him standing with Elliot in the communicating doorway when she went in. She knew too, when Cecil Glover turned and angrily strode out, that, as he had said he would, he had reported her for being impudent to one of the directors.

She was ready to be called to account. Instead, after a moment or two spent in grim-faced study of her unrepentant expression, Elliot did no more than quietly close his door, and shut her from his view.

All that afternoon she expected to be summoned for a carpeting. But at five o'clock that call had still not come. Kacie took herself off home unable to believe that he intended to take Cecil Glover's complaint no further!

The first sound heard in her flat the next morning, was a sneeze. Her cold had arrived. Kacie got out of bed, but felt too grim to be concerned with anything but getting herself bathed and dressed, and to her place of work.

At lunch time she again resorted to the aspirin bottle, and, although she did not have a clock-watching bone in her body, she prayed for five o'clock.

Oddly, when there was not a glimmer of anything remotely amusing on her horizon that day, she was again to feel her sense of humour matching Elliot's.

It was around four when, back from a meeting, he was near her desk just as she sneezed. She was in no mood for his unsympathetic comments.

'If you pass that cold on . . .' he started to threaten.

'We should get that close!' she smartly retorted. Then, 'Oh!' she exclaimed, and flicked him a glance to see that he too, had remembered just how close they had been.

It was all there in the raised eyebrow; in the sardonic amusement which played around his mouth. As humour started to curve her lips, perverse memory arrived to remind her that he had something of an objection to her smiles.

'I—er—must have caught a chill or something standing around while you inspected Dougal Aitken's invention,' she said in a hurried attempt to get back to the usual atmosphere. 'It was bitterly cold in that workshop,' she added.

Kacie saw his brow come down. And there was no sign of amusement, sardonic or any other when, as he continued into his own office, he offered a sarcastic: 'You noticed! From my observations, I'd have sworn you were too busy flirting with Aitken junior to be aware of the cold.'

Anger flared, but any retort she might have made to his departing back was lost in the urgency of having to find her handkerchief. But she was still angry enough to take him at his word when the sound of her sneezes died and an irritated voice from the inner sanctum bellowed, 'For God's sake—go home.'

She felt worse than ever when she dragged herself out of bed the next morning. But with the thought of how she must catch up on yesterday's work before she started today's she somehow got herself to the office for nine.

Elliot looked up when she went in, but she could find no cheery greeting for him. Though she was very conscious as she removed the cover from her typewriter, that he had left his office and was on his way to have a word with her.

As she looked up and he took in her washed out face, he asked 'What do you think you're doing here?'

Her muzzy head left her with little ability to work out riddles. 'I work here!' she replied, her sore throat making her voice more of a croak.

'Not today, you don't,' he replied firmly. 'Nor, by the look and sound of you, for the rest of the week.'

'But . . .' she started to croak.

'Do I take time out to return you from whence you came—or do you go under your own steam?' he asked, his tone almost friendly. For no accountable reason Kacie felt tears come to her eyes.

He would never forgive her if she did anything so drippy as to collapse into tears at his few kind words.

She took a second out to pull herself together and to decide that her cold had a lot to answer for.

'Well, if you put it like that,' she said, and replaced her typewriter cover. And, whether he disliked her smiles or not, she smiled, and gave in to the lovely thought of going back to bed.

Throughout that Wednesday, she alternately slept, sneezed, coughed, and dosed herself with aspirin. She awoke from another doze to find it was five o'clock, and her thoughts went automatically to the office, but more particularly, to Elliot Quantrell. She fell asleep again, with Elliot on her mind.

The ringing of the telephone saw her surfacing around seven to drag on her housecoat, and to go and answer it.

'You sound bad,' opined Susan Baylis on hearing her croaky voice. Kacie told her she had a bit of a cold, and Sue exclaimed, 'Oh good!' then quickly, 'I didn't mean about your cold,' and went on to explain. 'You weren't at the club last night, so I—um—sort of wondered if you were feeling a little—um—awkward about coming. You know—after letting the side down last weekend.'

More fully awake, Kacie wondered then if she should rechristen her 'bit of a cold'—amnesia. For she had forgotten all about the club, and only then did it dawn on her, how, since she had gone to Scotland with Elliot, she had barely given a thought to badminton, or to the team!

'How did the tournament go?' She thought she had better make up for lost time.

'We won!' squealed Sue. 'Can you believe it? Simon and I won!' There followed a shuttlecock by shuttlecock account, during which Kacie manoeuvred herself into an easy chair, now and then interjecting with a word or two of her own.

Sue asked if she would come to the club tomorrow, and on hearing she was off work and thought she would stay indoors for a while, remarked, 'Simon won't be there either. He's playing a singles match somewhere else.' A thought suddenly struck, and she brightened, 'I say,' she enthused, 'if you're confined indoors, why don't I come over tomorrow after work? I can pick up a Chinese meal for us both on my way,' she warmed to the idea, 'and I can tell you all about the tournament then.'

Kacie thought she had just heard all about the tournament. But since Sue was obviously at a loose end with Simon not going to the club tomorrow, she said she would welcome having someone to talk with, and Sue rang off.

Kacie remained where she was for a minute or two after Sue's call. She sneezed, blew her nose and contemplated which she wanted the more—to return to bed, or a cup of tea.

Tea, she decided. But before she had left her chair, her door bell rang. She surmised that a neighbour wanted a quick word about something, and, aware she looked a wreck, she went to the door. It wasn't a neighbour standing there, but none other than Elliot Quantrell.

'Er—H-hello,' she said startled, her greeting, even to her ears, sounding idiotic, her thoughts quickly transferring to what a mess her hair must look. 'C-come in,' she invited semi-automatically, her thoughts taken up with the scrubbed schoolgirl sight she must appear without her usual light application of make-up.

As he accepted her invitation and turned to close the door, she realised that she was behaving just like some schoolgirl too. Kacie endeavoured to right the situation.

She was striving hard to attain the appearance of a

fully composed secretary, when he finished his brief
scan of her tidy sitting-room, and his eyes settled on
her. But she knew it was going to be uphill work when
his eyes went from her flowing red hair to take in her
pale green robe. How could she adopt a cool mantle
when she stood before him in her nightdress?

She tried just the same, and was about to ask if his
call was because of difficulty in locating some file or
other, when he enquired, 'How did your day go?'

'I slept most of it away.'

'Have you eaten?' he asked.

'I'm . . .' She broke off to dive into her robe pocket
for her handkerchief, sneezed, and then thought her
sneeze must have rattled her brains. Because, when
she continued with her reply and told him, 'I'm not
hungry,' she found she also tacked on, 'I was just
going to make a cup of tea—would you like one?

Her surprises for the day were not yet over. Elliot
was always so busy that she was sure somewhere in his
brain were inscribed the words 'Never leave until
tomorrow what you can do today'.

She expected a curt refusal. But instead he told her
almost kindly, 'Hop into bed, I'll make it.'

She sat where he had sent her, listening to the
sounds of him sorting out her cups and saucers. She
could only suppose that shock was responsible for the
fact that when he had left her in order to hunt up her
kitchen, she had stared after him for only a moment,
and then, totally without protest, she had obeyed his
instructions.

She was a little more collected when, bearing a tray
of tea for two, he came into her bedroom. Of course he
had not popped in solely on the off-chance that she
might want a cup of tea. She again thought to ask if
there was some file mislaid.

Then the question was taken completely from her

head. Because he set the tray aside, and, while her heart seemed to stop, he bent over her, his arms reaching down for her.

'Your tea's going to embroider the sheets, if you sit like that,' he said and his hands adjusted the pillows at her back.

Her breathing was laboured. His chest was so near to her face, and with an arm either side of her she could feel the strength of his hard muscled arms. Suddenly, she was overwhelmingly conscious of his virile maleness. Hoping to get clear of the sensations which engulfed her, she lifted her head. But in doing so, her face brushed against him; and in those few short seconds, Kacie felt as if her entire being was dominated by him.

When he pulled back and one of his hands accidentally feathered her shoulder, an electrified tingle shot through her whole body and Kacie knew a total awareness of him. She looked up, and then found it hard to breathe at all. For the warm grey eyes that met hers, were reflecting nothing, but a similar complete tingling awareness—of her!

Elliot paused, and stared into her green eyes, and Kacie, her heart pounding beneath her ribs, knew he was going to kiss her. When his eyes slid down to her mouth, she was sure of it.

But, when she knew she wanted his kiss, he straightened away from her. As if satisfied he could now hand over her tea without the risk or mishap, he turned to the tray, and handed her a cup and saucer.

Her heart drummed and she knew a fear that he might have read how much she had wanted him to kiss her. She sought hard to find some everyday remark to show she had been entirely unaffected by his nearness. But it was he who spoke first.

Looking completely at ease in the chair he had

pulled up to the bed, he sat back and observed, 'D'you know, Kacie Peters, even with a pink tip to your nose, you look terrific.'

The tension in her broke and she had to laugh. For all his throw-away remark had been of a personal nature, it had been quite impersonally put. Her world had righted itself, but she still had a smile on her face when, just as easily, she tossed back, 'If that remark was designed to make me feel better than the wreck I know I look, Elliot Quantrell—it does.'

It was his turn to laugh, and Kacie's heart fluttered at how, when he put his stern face away, his laughter look made him human and somehow endearing.

Abruptly she caught herself up short as if to avoid some truth that was knocking on her door.

'How did business go today?'

Elliot placed his empty cup down on the tray and stood up. 'Not as smoothly as I'd have liked,' he replied, and then gave her a lop-sided grin as he added, 'I confess, I've missed your efficient presence.'

He did not stay long after his admission he found her efficient. After ordering her not to come into the office before Monday, he went on his way—leaving Kacie with a fair bit of soul searching to do.

It was not her efficient secretarial skills she wanted him to miss, but her, Kacie Peters. She was attracted to him. That, in itself, was enough to keep her awake well past her usual time for slumber. As one thought chased after another, she was wide awake for hours.

She remembered how she thought Elliot had been about to kiss her; and how she had wanted his kiss. She remembered the time she had slapped him, and he *had* kissed her. She had been attracted to him then, without even knowing it, she realised. Why else had she stopped struggling, and enjoyed the feel of his mouth over hers!

That was why she had been so discomfited to open
her door and to see him so unexpectedly standing
there. That attraction she felt for him, even if she had
not recognised it at the time, decreed he should not see
her looking as though she had just been pulled
through a hedge backwards.

Why, or how, that attraction had grown, was a
mystery to her. In that first week she had felt she hated
him. He was so unlike her ex-boss, Vincent Jenner.

It was a shock to discover how long it was since she
had given Vincent a thought. I don't love Vincent, she
realised with a start. I never did love him! Not in the
way I thought I did anyhow. It had taken the move
from Vincent and the job with Elliot, to show her how
she had been deceived in thinking she loved Vincent.

With overwhelming clarity, Kacie saw then that all
she felt for Vincent, was affection. Affection which
over the years had been warmed by the sympathy she
felt for the tangle his marriage was in. Her sensitivity
to his frailties had somehow built up, so that in her
last six months of working for him, she had believed
mistakenly, that she loved him.

That mistaken belief had been the reason for her
leaving him. But she had not missed him nearly as
much as she had thought she would. Nor had it taken
long for her not to miss him at all. In fact, she could
not remember the last time she had given him *this*
much thought!

Her eyelids started to droop, and her thoughts of
Vincent and Elliot grew confused. But, as sleep came
to claim her, there was no confusion in her mind about
one subject. There had been no reason whatsoever for
her to leave Jenner Products. Yet, even though, from
comments he had made, she knew Vincent would be
pleased to re-employ her; there was no going back.
Not now. Not now that she had worked with Elliot.

CHAPTER FIVE

THERE was no doubt in her mind the following morning, that all she felt for Vincent Jenner was an affection for the nice person he was. But if Kacie could truthfully deny a love for Vincent, she could not as truthfully deny the attraction she felt for Elliot.

Her cold was much improved, but since she saw no sense in going to work only to be sent straight back home again, she had plenty of time in which to dwell on her employer. It did not take her long to see that if she was to be allowed to keep her job, she was going to have to keep any attraction she felt for Elliot very well hidden.

Elliot had made no bones about telling her he never mixed business with pleasure. Even if he was attracted to her in return, which he wasn't, he would stamp down hard on that attraction . . . Suddenly, her heart gave a lurch, and her thoughts stopped abruptly as she considered her wildest notion yet—was Elliot attracted to her?

He had kissed her, she recalled. But he had only kissed her because there was something bred in him which had prevented him slapping her back when she had taken a swipe at him.

He had called to see her last night, hadn't he? He had made no mention of a missing file or a missing anything else, had he? In fact, business had hardly received a mention.

Kacie warmed to her theme when she remembered how, to her amazement, he had made her a cup of tea! She was sure too that he had wanted to kiss her when he adjusted her pillows.

She had still not got the absurd notion out of her head when afternoon arrived. Maybe Elliot had decided against kissing her, she even found herself thinking, because he did not have time to spare to be away from the office if he caught her cold.

She *was* absurd, she realised in the next moment. By the mere fact he had been in the same room, he had already taken the risk of catching her cold.

Aware that her crazy notion was built on the weakest of foundations, she finally gave up her silent debate. Not from anything she said, or from any glance she gave, was Elliot Quantrell going to know of the romantic stirrings he had aroused in her, she decided.

Then the phone rang, and it was Elliot enquiring about something she had been dealing with, and Kacie's heart was supercharged again.

'You sound better,' he observed when she had passed over the information he required, 'if still a shade breathless.'

'I'm much, much better,' she said, and blatantly lied, 'you caught me at the tail end of a coughing bout.'

'Have you had anything to eat today?' he asked.

'A little,' she told him. Then, thinking that he might be worried on that score, she hurried to add, 'A friend is coming round tonight with a take-away. You know how those Chinese meals fill . . .'

Anger flared to life when she found she was talking to a dead line. Rude swine, she railed. But why she should think he would be any different from the way he always was at the office? He didn't have time to listen to a monologue about the filling contents of crispy noodles.

If there was a hiccup in office procedure during the following day, it was handled without Elliot needing to telephone her again.

By Monday, Kacie was over her cold, but would have gone to work even if it had decided to linger. She took extra care with her appearance, and knew a feeling of excitement which had nothing to do with anticipating a day which she knew in advance would see no easy workload.

Inside the Quantrell building with ample time to spare to be at her desk before nine, she was first buttonholed by Mike Carey. Mike was in no hurry to go to his office, but appeared to have all day in which to tell her how like a morgue the place had been without her.

'Kind of you to say so, Mike,' she said lightly. 'But I must get on—I expect I'll have a lot of catching up to do.'

Within yards of her office, she met Jonathan Davy coming the other way. 'They tell me you've been off sick, but I don't believe it,' he stated, and, his eyes going over the look of her in her best sage-green suit, 'You look as good as ever,' he declared.

'I'm feeling as good as ever.' She smiled, and was just about to add the same departing line when, without a word, Elliot strode past the two of them. 'See you,' she said quickly.

She caught up with Elliot as he was opening the office door. But she could tell from the dark expression which appraised her, that it wasn't in his mind to ask if she was recovered.

His greeting on her first morning back, was the short, pithy, comment: 'If you're fit enough to make it with my directors—you're fit enough to work.'

Kacie glared at his back when, leaving her to follow in behind him, he strode through her office and into his own domain, and shut her out.

She was still sending hate vibes at his door, when sounds reached her to let her know he was on the telephone. When the muffled speech ceased, she stayed where she was. She was damned if she would go through before she was called.

So a morning began when she was soon too involved to have a moment in which to discover which was the more potent—the magnetism he held, or the hate in her that warred against that attraction.

Had she still nursed any idea that the attraction was in any way mutual, it would have been shattered when, a few minutes before one, the outer door opened and a woman, who was the last word in sophistication, entered.

As if Kacie was entirely beneath her notice, the elegant fur-clad blonde walked straight past her, and leaving a wake of perfumed air, made a bee-line for Elliot's door.

'Do you have an appointment?' Kacie recovered from the shock and galvanised herself to action to reach the door before the haughty blonde could sail through it.

'Appointment?' queried the highly glossed mouth, about the only feature in the painted face to move.

'Mr Quantrell prefers not to be interrupted . . .' Kacie broke off, for suddenly the door was open, and Elliot stood there.

'Your little run-around is quite possessive of your time, darling,' the blonde immediately drawled. 'I'm sure she'd have flattened herself against the woodwork rather than let me interrupt you.'

What reply Elliot made, Kacie never heard. For emotions were storming through her which had her too stunned to pick up a word. It did not help when, without so much as a glance in her direction, she saw him escort the blonde to the outer door. The woman's words floated back, 'Have you booked a table at my favourite restaurant, Elliot darling?'

The outer door closed, and Kacie was suddenly bereft of appetite. Without any awareness that she had moved, she found she was at her desk and that she had collapsed on to her chair.

Gradually the first shock of the revelation which had just come to her, began to recede. But there was no escape from the knowledge, unpalatable though it was, that the emotion which had so violently attacked her when she heard the blonde call Elliot 'darling', had been nothing but pure jealousy.

It was not simple attraction she felt for Elliot—but love!

She knew it, and recognised it, even while she tried to tell herself that this emotion was nothing like any feeling she had ever felt before. What she had felt for Vincent was tepid by comparison.

Unable to stay put, she grabbed up her shoulder bag, and went to a nearby park. But she could not get away from the truth which had come unannounced, and so totally unwanted.

My God, she thought, when the picture of Elliot with the blonde woman refused to be ejected, I must have been more semi-delirious than light-headed! How could I ever have thought Elliot might be attracted—even in the tiniest way—to me!

Attracted! My heavens, what had got into her! She had no need to look beyond the elegant, sophisticated blonde to know what type of woman attracted him.

Fidgety still, Kacie left her park bench and, with her mind full of Elliot, turned her feet towards her office. That, when he was such a demon for work, he should drop everything the instant the snooty blonde appeared, spoke volumes in her sad opinion.

His sophisticated woman friend had referred disdainfully to her as his 'little run-around'. But before she could begin to be riled about that, the blonde had gone on to call him 'darling' in that familiar way, and all hell had broken loose inside her.

What hurt her most was the memory of how Elliot had escorted the condescending woman out to lunch without so much as a glance in her direction. It was obvious to Kacie then, that far from being attracted to her, she was so beneath his notice, she might just as well be a piece of his office machinery.

In one way, it was a relief when he was late coming back from lunch. She had looked at her watch not once but a dozen times as she listened for his return. But the hour and fifty-three minutes before she saw him again, gave her time in which to decide not to do anything hasty.

Her initial reaction was to hand in her notice the moment he showed his face. Minutes later, she knew she could not do anything of the kind. While she admitted it most unlikely he would look beneath the surface of why she should so suddenly want to leave, she could not risk it. They did not come much smarter than him, and since the day—until the blonde's arrival—had gone on much the same as normal, Kacie saw she must not give him scope to connect her resignation with his woman-friend.

In her heart, Kacie knew she did not want to leave anyway. If he wanted an office machine, that's precisely what she would be, she resolved, when he walked in.

So much for being a machine, whispered her brain when just knowing that he was there set her pulses racing. Determinedly, she carried on typing, her fingers tapping out a line that didn't make sense in any language, when he halted at her desk. She took her fingers from the keys, and looked up.

Elliot was all smiles. 'For future reference,' he

informed her, his voice all pleasantness and light showing, if she didn't already know it, that someone had put him in a good humour, 'Mrs Neasom can interrupt me any time.'

'I'll make a note,' Kacie replied as any efficient secretary would. But some devil she did not know she possessed pushed at her and she could not resist asking while maintaining her 'perfect secretary' expression, 'Would Mrs Neasom be the—lady—who called just before lunch?'

In her opinion, a lady would have better manners than the blonde. But if Elliot noticed her slight hesitation before she used the word, it did not show.

'The same,' he replied evenly. 'Lana Neasom is a—close friend.'

With that, he carried on to his office, and Kacie, the devil in her beaten to a pulp by his last comment, took out the gibberish she had just typed, and started again.

Elliot's good humour had darts of jealousy spearing her with every affable utterance he made during the next two hours. Never had she thought she would welcome a return of the curt, concise authoritarian he usually was. As five o'clock neared, she owned it would have been preferable to the knowledge that some other woman had more power to sweeten him that she did.

Her pride made her pretend she did not care. But, with the communicating door left open, she only had to catch a glimpse of him, to know from the upsurge of emotion which swamped her, that she did care. She was in love with him, she could not deny, and being in love, she discovered, was a vastly different emotion from infatuation, or simple affection.

Just before five, much to her surprise, Gavin Aitken, of all people, rang. But that Gavin had taken it into his head to ring her from Scotland was not her only surprise. No sooner were the preliminaries out of the way, than he asked:

'Are you better?' Before she could reply, he was saying, 'I only rang on the off chance. When Elliot told me you were off sick, I didn't expect you to be in work today.'

'Elliot told y . . .' Her voice faded when her glance through the open doorway showed her employer had looked up on hearing her speak his first name. But Gavin was going on to reproach her.

'You'd forgotten all about me coming to London last weekend.'

'No, no I hadn't,' she lied quickly, and took her eyes from Elliot to try to wake up her brain. 'How did the wedding go?'

'The stag night was better,' he replied, immediately cheered that she had remembered. 'Though I'd have got out of that if I could have taken you out to dinner last Friday.'

'You came to London last Friday?' she enquired, more for something to say than anything else.

'Late Thursday, as a matter of fact,' he replied. 'But when I rang in the hope of making some arrangement for Friday, Elliot told me you were ill.'

That Elliot had not told her of Gavin's call, was, she thought, no more than could be expected. He had far more important things on his mind—Lana Neasom, for example.

'I'm sorry I missed seeing you, Gavin,' she roused herself to tell him. 'Though with me sneezing and spluttering all over the place, perhaps it was just as well.'

'I don't know about that,' he answered warmly. 'But when Elliot refused to give me your address, or even your home number and told me you needed to rest all you could, I realised you must be quite poorly.'

'I—it's—er—marvellous what modern medicines can do, isn't it,' she murmured, not completely sure—when Elliot wouldn't give a damn anyway—why she should cover for him.

'Are you certain you're fit enough to be in work today?' Gavin enquired.

'Quite certain,' she told him, not wanting a detailed discussion on her health. 'This call must be costing you a bomb,' she reminded him.

'You'll make some man a thrifty wife,' he teased. 'How about letting me have your home number, then I can ring you during the cheap rate?'

Kacie saw no reason not to give him her phone number, conscious as she did so that Elliot would recognise it.

'Do I have to wait all day for those figures?' Elliot barked the moment she came off the phone, and all thoughts of asking why he had told Gavin she was at death's door went from her head.

Pardon me for living, she thought. Mutinous on the instant, loving him and hating him both at the same time, she ripped the typed page from her typewriter and took it to him.

Strangely, when she had wanted him to be his same unlovable, bossy self, that did not please her either.

Things were back to normal on Tuesday. That was to say, Elliot was the same as if Lana Neasom had never shown her lovely painted face inside the office, and Kacie, outwardly, coped with an unflappability which was becoming part and parcel of her being his secretary. What went on inside her, however, was a totally different matter. For she had soon discovered, that by wishing not to be in love with him, she was on a hiding to nothing. Love just did not work like that.

With Elliot so constantly in her mind, Kacie realised that in the interests of sanity, she had better find herself something else to think about. To that end, poor second though it was, she roused herself that evening and collected up her badminton gear.

'You're out of practice,' was Simon's pronouncement when thoughts of Elliot came between her and her game and resulted in her having played abominably.

'You could be right,' she replied, and went home to think of her employer and to wonder if it would not be better if she gave in her notice.

She was still toying with the idea as she drove to work on Wednesday. But when, with the post out of the way, Elliot told her he wanted everything cleared up that night; and went on to say he would not be in the office for the next two days, Kacie knew that 'toying' with the idea was all it was.

'You have business elsewhere?' she enquired, her expression cool, while her insides were in torment. If he was to be away tomorrow and the day after, then she would not see him before Monday! That would make it four whole days before she saw him again!

'If you've no objection,' he replied, at his sarcastic best.

'None whatsoever,' she answered, just biting down the words 'I consider it a bonus' which rose to her tongue at his uncalled-for sarcasm.

'Get me a seat on the first flight tomorrow for Brussels,' he instructed.

'Returning Friday?' she queried.

He nodded, and would have proceeded straight away into some other business, only just then, the most exciting and wonderful thought suddenly came to Kacie.

'You're going on your own?' she spurted in to ask.

His right eyebrow ascending aloft as suddenly dashed her hopes. She realised what he thought she was asking, and jealousy gnawed at her, so that she grabbed a tight hold on all the coolness she could muster.

'I wasn't enquiring if you intend to take a—close friend—for company,' she told him stonily, while hoping for hurricane flying conditions on the morrow, 'merely wanting to know—since you required a secretary with you the last time you were away from the office on business—if you intend to leave it until five tonight to tell me to cancel the heavy date I have for tomorrow.'

'Keep your heavy date,' Elliot snarled, his face like thunder.

Kacie booked a flight ticket for one.

Thursday, without him in the office, was a day filled with aching gaps. She knew by then, that in company with interested parties from several countries, Elliot was in Brussels to look at some embryonic feat of engineering which, if all went well, should ultimately prove a world first.

Despite telling him she had a heavy date that evening, she had nothing planned. But at the end of the day, with Monday light years away, she took herself off to the badminton club desperate to kill time. She played another terrible game.

Friday at work, was a repeat of the day before, with the only consolation at the close of day, that Monday had come nearer.

When Saturday lunch time came around her spirits were lower than low. The morning dragged by on leaden feet. This was the first weekend since she had discovered her love for Elliot. Future weekends, with her contact broken with him Friday to Monday, were not going to be any better.

What she was going to feel like when he went on his imminent trip to Canada for four whole weeks, she

dared not to think. But the fact he had taken himself
off to Brussels without a secretary, put an end to any
idea that he might want her to accompany him across
the Atlantic. His former secretary was working at the
Canadian division, and could well fill in if needed. Not
to mention the fact that there must be any number of
well-trained secretaries employed by the company
over there.

When common sense ordered that she should eat,
Kacie made herself a meal she had no appetite for. She
was washing up when she remembered it was her turn
to phone her mother. For the next few minutes, afraid
any flatness might be picked up by her parent, she
concentrated on finding just the right bright and
breezy tone to make her call.

She had her hand on the phone, when, suddenly, it
rang. She lifted the receiver. 'Come and pick me up,'
said Elliot without preamble, and even though he
sounded grumpy, the sun had all at once burst
through her clouded sky.

With her heart fluttering wildly, she thought she
should perhaps tell him she had better things to do on
her day off than to jump to his bidding. But that was
before the heaven-sent thought came that, were she
her male counterpart, she might well say 'Yes sir.
Three bags full sir'. In any case, she was just longing
for the sight of him.

'Certainly,' she replied, holding down the bright
tone which she had earlier had to seek hard to find.
'Where are you?' she enquired, lighting on the
possibility he had lunched at his club and then found
his car with a double puncture.

'At the airport,' he told her shortly, and abruptly
hung up, leaving her to wonder why, when he should
have returned from Brussels yesterday, he had stayed
over an extra night.

Jealousy had her almost deciding that he could jolly well stew at the airport. In her mind's eye she visualised Elliot being entertained by a Belgian version of Lana Neasom. His plane reservation would be incidental if he decided to take some beauty to dinner, and then, stay over . . .

Jealousy was beaten back when her yearning just to see him took over. She took pointless minutes to change into her Sunday best, only to change back again into her trousers and sweater. It would be better, she thought, if he saw she had come as she was when he had rung, and had not seen any reason to bother to change.

Kacie thought it was fortunate that it was quite a long drive from her flat to the airport. She was going to need every minute of the journey to be ready to show Elliot her cool unruffled secretarial self when she arrived.

She had assumed that he would drive himself to and from the airport. Though with his car being expensive, and the last word in design, perhaps he had not wanted to leave it parked at the airport during his absence.

She fully expected to see him stomping impatiently about when she reached her destination. When he was nowhere to be seen, she investigated all cafeterias and the like, without success, then went to make enquiries.

Directed to a private annexe, her unflappable front started to desert her. But when she located the door to the room where she knew she would find him, Kacie hauled her efficient secretary image up from off the floor, then tapped lightly on the panelling and went in.

Elliot had his back to the door, and did not turn around.

'Sorry for the delay,' said Kacie, striving for a cool tone. 'I wasn't sure where to find . . .' She broke off as he looked round. Goodness, she thought, observing the lack of colour in his face, is he hung-over!

The dark glasses he wore, confirmed it. For when there was not so much as a ray of sunshine about that day—it was plain he could not stand even the dimmest of artificial or neutral light.

'Let's get going,' he said, picking up his case, his voice short, impatient, and that of a man whom Kacie already knew was unaccustomed to having to wait for anything.

'Did you have a successful trip?' she forced herself to ask. The grunt she received for an answer might well have deflated her, had not Elliot sent her insides all of a tremor when possessively as they went out to her car, he took hold of her elbow.

She unlocked her car and half expected him to insist he would do the driving. But when without a word he handed her his case and got into the passenger seat, Kacie stowed his luggage, then got behind the steering wheel.

'Where to?' she asked.

'Home,' he grunted, and leant his head on the head rest, to give her the impression he would be catching up on his missed sleep before she learned where his home was. 'Ashwith, in Berkshire,' he added, sounding weary, but managed to keep awake for long enough to give her a few general directions.

Kacie started up the car with the disgruntled thought that he had lived it up so much last night, he had probably not been to bed at all. Or, if he had been to bed . . . She halted the thought before it went further, knowing she had no right whatsoever to be jealous of a thing he did.

For the most part it was a silent drive. She had good navigational instincts, but, with little sympathy for her hung-over employer, she did not mind in the least waking him when she had doubts over which road to take. Though because these days she never thought of him as Mr Quantrell, she forgot herself when she nudged his arm to rouse him.

'Wake up, Elliot, if you don't want to get lost.'

'Elliot,' he informed her shortly, 'was not asleep.'

Liar, she thought. His eyes behind those thick dark lenses had been closed, she was sure of it.

'Which way now?' she asked, her voice cool.

She guessed he must have the mother and father of all headaches if the best he could do was to growl directions. But, since it wasn't her fault, she didn't see why she should accept the blame when, in the drive of the impressive looking Ashwith Court, he bumped into her as she handed him his case, then rounded on her and told her to look where the hell she was going.

'If you took your sun glasses off, then maybe you'd see where *you* were going,' she snapped.

'You'd better come in for some refreshment after your drive,' he told her uninvitingly. 'My housekeeper will fix you up with a cup of tea or something.'

Pride stormed in to squash her desire to see inside his home, and to study a side more personal than their office surrounds. If he thought he could take her inside Ashwith Court and then dump her with his housekeeper—not that she had anything against housekeepers—he had another think coming.

'I have to wash my hair before I go out tonight,' she told him tartly. 'I'd better get back.'

So much for his half-hearted invitation, Kacie fumed, for he did not insist. She was glad she would not see him again until Monday. Yet, as he stood tight lipped and watched her as she got into her car, she knew that he would no sooner be out of her sight, than she would be aching to see him again.

Kacie drove back to her flat thinking she must have

been mad to have got herself into a state when he had
telephoned her from the airport. Not so much as a
thank you had come her way for going to fetch him!
Not that she wanted his thanks. But it hurt just the
same to know that he thought of her as just another
office machine.

CHAPTER SIX

As she knew she would, Kacie drove to her office on Monday with an inner excitement—soon, the long aching hours since she had last seen Elliot, would be over.

She had given up wondering about this nonsense-person that love had made of her. Recalling the foul mood he had been in on Saturday, she should be driving to the office mutinying about the swine she had the misfortune to work for; instead of which, she just could not wait to get there.

She was the first to arrive and sat down to begin the day's business. Surely he was over his giant sized hangover by now! Unwanted darts of jealousy tried to defeat her when, unbidden, thoughts returned of how he had come to earn such debility which took colour from his face, and which called for dark glasses. Firmly Kacie beat away jealous pin-pricks. Elliot would soon be here.

But Elliot didn't arrive. At nine-thirty there was still no sign of him and Kacie began to get worried. There could be a hundred and one different reasons for him being late, she told herself, but she could not dismiss visions of him, excellent driver though she knew he was, lying hurt in a car smash somewhere.

Snow had been forecast, she remembered. A country girl herself, she knew all about drifts which made some rural roads impassable. Elliot lived in the country didn't he? Perhaps the village of Ashwith was already snowbound.

Her panicking emotions started to get on top of her.

Surely he would have got to the nearest telephone and . . .

At that very moment, the phone rang. With unquestioning certainty, she just knew it would be him. But the instinct to yank up the phone and urgently ask if he was all right, had to be suppressed. Elliot had heard her answer the phone many times— she must try and find that same telephone manner.

'Kacie?' he questioned when, the phone in her hand, no words would come.

'El . . . Mr Quantrell?' she replied, so pleased to hear him as aggressive as usual at being kept waiting. Quickly she reached for her note pad and efficient manner. 'You've been delayed?' she enquired evenly.

'I'm working from home today,' he said crisply. 'Get over here with . . .'

'You're ill?' The question shot from her, her even manner gone. 'What's wrong?' she asked, urgency refusing to be suppressed.

'For God's sake stop flapping,' he barked irritably. 'You know where I live. Bring with you the Darlington and Brew file. I'll need the . . .'

Automatically her fingers flew over her pad as she took down this file and that file, so that by the time he had finished giving his orders, she was to wonder if it might not be simpler to remove his whole office to Ashwith Court. But if that was a bit of an exaggeration, it was plain to Kacie that, for whatever reason, it would not be just for today her employer would be working from his home.

'You'll want me to cancel your appointm . . .'

'Davy's secretary will do that. He's taking over,' Elliot grunted, to let her know he had already spoken with Jonathan Davy. As ever he was short with his commands, not a 'can you' or a 'will you' in sight. 'I want you here—now,' he barked, and hung up.

'Yes sir, no sir, any time you say, sir,' Kacie said to the silent receiver as she replaced it in its cradle. But her spurt of annoyance with him did not last. Before she could start to wonder what the dickens was going on, Jonathan Davy's thin bespectacled secretary was there.

'I've been sent to photostat a couple of relevant pages from Mr Quantrell's desk diary before you take it,' she explained, 'and also to offer any assistance you might need.'

A half an hour later, with a typewriter carried out to her car by a messenger, her car loaded with the files Elliot had requested, and with the day's post in a folder on the seat beside her, Kacie set off.

It was the first chance she'd had, since Elliot's phone call, to draw breath. But she did not hang about. As soon as she was clear of London, down went her foot on the accelerator—her thoughts went at about the same pace.

He must be ill, she thought, in panic. She calmed down when she reasoned that Elliot could not be so desperately ill. To judge by what she had brought with her, he intended to continue in his workaholic ways.

If he was still suffering from his monumental hangover then he must have really painted the Belgian capital red while he was out there, Kacie concluded and again batted away jealous thoughts.

On she travelled. The sky was heavily laden, but so far, not one flake of snow had fallen, therefore she eliminated her theory of Elliot working from home because he was blocked in by snow. In any case, if Ashwith were snowbound, it would be equally impossible for her to get to him.

Kacie did not know a moment's peace on that drive. By the time she drew up at Ashwith Court, she had

wished many times that she had forgotten her pride
and asked Jonathan Davy's secretary what exactly was
happening.

Loaded with files, with the post folder on top, she
went up the stone steps, and manoeuvred her hands
and their burden until she had a free finger with which
to ring the doorbell.

A smart, if severe-looking lady answered the door.
'You must be Miss Peters,' she said on observing
Kacie standing there with files up to her chin. 'Come
in,' she invited, her voice showing all the warmth
which her expression lacked. 'I'm Mrs Watts, Mr
Quantrell's housekeeper,' she introduced herself as
Kacie stepped into the wide plush hall.

'I'm sorry I can't shake hands,' Kacie apologised,
and smiled over the top of her cargo.

'Mr Quantrell said I was to show you to the study
when you arrived,' Mrs Watts told her. 'If you'd like
to come this way,' she added.

'Mr . . .' Kacie bit back the question of was Mr
Quantrell all right when the housekeeper, obviously
thinking she was following, did not hear, and led the
way to one of the doors down the hall.

Kacie's heart had already started to drum, but it
took a giddy leap when, after a discreet tap, Mrs Watts
pushed open the door for her and Kacie saw Elliot
seated at his study desk.

He did not rise from his chair when she went in, not
that she expected him to. But just the fact he still had
need of those dark glasses quietened the giddy
sensation in her heart and concern for him took over.

So far he had not even glanced her way, which gave
her time to hide her concern under a cloak of
efficiency, as she told him, 'I think I've brought about
everything with me, but the kitchen sink.'

'You took your time getting here,' he replied

tersely—an indication his mood had not sweetened while he waited for her to arrive.

Her concern started to ebb, for to be so accused when she had gone as fast as she could to get to him, told her that he was his usual vitriolic office self.

She noted there was ample space on his desk to unload her cargo. Without saying another word she moved over to it and began to put down the files she carried. She then took the post folder from the top.

As she placed the folder down on another empty space, that concern flooded in again. Without knowing what it was, Kacie knew something was wrong.

A wrinkle appeared on her otherwise smooth brow but, not wanting her ears blistered when Elliot's patience ran out, she went to bring a chair from the far wall and take it to the desk so they could begin.

She knew from past experience that she stood to get shot down in flames if she dared ask him what was wrong, she had just put her hand to the chair-back when suddenly, she thought she had the answer, and stilled.

When, if ever, had she seen so much spare space on his desk! Indeed, from the way he liked to have his papers spread about him, she had more than once thought that they just didn't make a desk so large that he could not cover it.

Agitation started to get to her. Elliot was not the type to sit in idleness. The cut and thrust of business were meat and drink to him. At the office or at home, he would find some plan to formulate, some campaign to map out. Yet, with a good part of the morning gone while he waited for her to arrive—he had not so much as uncapped his fountain pen!

'Is it your intention to stand around decorating my study all day, or may we get on with some work?

The brusque question had broken into her thoughts,

but for once his sarcasm did not even touch her. Gripping hard on to the chair, Kacie carried it to the side of his desk and sat down.

'I expect you'll want to clear this morning's post first,' she suggested as calmly as she could.

When she went to pass him the folder, he seemed to hesitate before curtly ordering:

'You read it. You deal with it.'

'Me!' she exclaimed, well able to deal with some matters, but aware she would be taking her life in her hands to attempt others.

'Dammit, woman!' he exploded, a world of frustration hitting her ears. 'What do I pay you for?' he bellowed.

'You don't pay me to make decisions which could cost the company millions, like whether or not I should reply in the affirmative to today's letter from Grieg and Box.' Kacie forgot her agitation to fire straight back, his unearned wrath causing her to ignore his fury when he made an angry movement and succeeded in knocking several bulky files flying from the desk.

A tense silence followed where she determined, since the grey files and their contents strewn over the matching grey carpet were nearer to him anyway, that she'd be damned if she would pick them up. He knocked them down, let him play paper chaser, she thought mutinously. It was bad enough that she had the job of re-filing everything into the correct order anyway.

Her rage did not last. After long silent seconds, Elliot regained control of his temper, and said quietly, 'Pick it up, Kacie.' It was her love for him that had her leaving her chair to comply.

She thought she had regained her calm when, the files back on the desk ready to be sorted out when she had a moment, she retook her seat. Then suddenly,

every scrap of her composure went. All at once it came
to her that there had not been one file littering the
floor, but several. Yet Elliot had spoken in the
singular. That, together with his request that she read
the mail made her strain her eyes, in a vain effort to
see beyond the dark lenses he had on. Every vestige of
colour slowly drained from her face, and her voice was
a shocked, disbelieving whisper.

'You—can't see!'

'I ...' he started to bite back aggressively. Then
that frustration which had coloured his voice before,
was suddenly apparent again, when he barked, 'So
now you know, you can damn well read me today's
correspondence.'

Reeling, she did nothing of the kind. More than
anything, as she coped with shock, she wanted to go to
him, to hold him. Kacie held back. Without having to
think about it, she knew Elliot would see her love only
as pity. And though she did pity him, she knew he
would take any sign of such an emotion as an insult.

By a mammoth effort, she stayed fast in her chair,
but she could not take the husky quality from her
voice, however hard she tried, when eventually she
managed to question, 'You've been—like this—since
Saturday! That's why you rang and asked me to
collect you from the airport.'

The angry line of his mouth advised that even
unsighted Elliot had more interest in getting down to
work, than he had in answering any of her questions.
But when she fully expected to be attacked by another
burst of his frustration, he did give her an answer—
albeit sarcastically.

'Since it appears we're going to get nothing done
until I've satisfied your morbid curiosity—I've been
like *this*, since Friday, when I got carted off to
hospital.'

'You've been in hospital!' she gasped, starting to hate herself for every one of her jealous thoughts. She had thought he had spent a wild old time last Friday. She had imagined him anywhere but a hospital bed—and all the time he had been confined to . . . Kacie swallowed on her anguish. 'You had an accident?' she asked, wanting to help him, but needing to know more.

'There was an accident,' he told her after a moment or two. 'It all happened so quickly. One moment I was totally involved, with my eyes fascinated by an intricate turning device, the next, some new formula cooling agent gave off a vapour which should have been safe—but it wasn't and from the moment it hit my eyes, they started stinging . . .'

Kacie had little engineering knowledge, but guessed that when metal cut metal at high speed, it had to be somehow cooled in the process. But none of that was of interest to her then, because her conscience was crucifying her as she remembered how last Saturday she had told him if he took his sunglasses off, then maybe he would see where he was going. It tormented her with guilt to remember how she had roared off so carelessly, and left him, a blind man—a man she loved with her whole being and whom she would protect like a wild cat if he ever had that sort of need—to find his own way into his home when he had not even known if he was facing the right way or not.

Appalled, Kacie could not live with her conscience. Swiftly she charged in to ask, 'Should you be out of hospital?'

'When I learned my only treatment was a few more days of eye drops every four hours, I saw no reason to stay put.' Elliot's reply was a cold dismissal of her concern.

Several questions presented themself all at once.

She chose the most important one of all. 'Are you . . . You're not . . .' She rephrased it, 'You're not going to be—permanently blind?'

'Good God, I hope not!' he replied with asperity which glanced off Kacie in her relief. 'Nor,' he added, 'am I unsighted now.'

'But—you couldn't see the files, or the papers which spilled on to the carpet just now!' she pointed out. 'You——'

'Enough!' He cut her off sharply. 'When the drops go in I can't see a damned thing. But the effects gradually wear off, so that by the time I'm due for the next lot I have most of my vision back although these lenses make colour less distinguishable. You, Miss Peters,' he told her, sounding at his most uncomplimentary, 'are now more of a shape than the blur you were when you first came in. Which means we must have been discussing something which is no concern of yours at least half an hour. Now,' he said curtly, 'since we have more important matters to get on with, read me the letter from Grieg and Box, and tell me when it gets to twelve o'clock noon.'

The fact that he had to rely on someone else to tell him the time made Kacie's heart ache, but in spite of the upsurge of compassion, as requested, she read him the letter.

She then discovered what it was like to work for a man who had short patience with personal affliction. His frustration in not being able to check things for himself was vented on the nearest person to hand— who just happened to be her.

She reminded him of the time at twelve, and was told abruptly, 'Go and tell Mrs Watts what you want for lunch.'

Caught out of her stride, Kacie expected him to add something else. But when for explanation he took a rubber bulb capped phial from his pocket, and she realised he did not want an audience while he administered his eye drops, she went looking for Mrs Watts.

'I'll lay a place for you in the dining-room,' said Mrs Watts, when Kacie had told her the pretext of her errand. 'I'll give you a call when I bring in Mr Quantrell's tray at one.'

'I could have a tray too,' Kacie told her, intending to save her the bother of laying up a table.

'Mr Quantrell ordered a tray especially,' the housekeeper replied, and added tactfully, 'I'm not sure he'll want anyone with him.'

Wishing she had realised for herself that Elliot would barely have learned his way round a lunch-plate and would, therefore, definitely not want company, Kacie returned to the study.

But if a fresh application of drops had made him totally unsighted, then she soon discovered that there was nothing whatsoever the matter with his acid tongue.

'Dare one hope,' he broke off in the middle of dictation to enquire, 'you've thought to bring a typewriter?'

'It's in my car,' she replied evenly, starting to feel the strain. 'It won't take me a min——'

'Stay put,' he commanded, 'I'll go and . . .' He broke off. 'Oh, God,' he breathed heavily, unable to go anywhere unaided.

'It isn't heavy,' she said quickly. She would have been ready then to bring in the cumbersome machine had it weighed two hundredweight.

'Leave it,' he grated, 'I'll get Joe to bring it in.'

For the rest of the time until Mrs Watts came to tell her her lunch was ready, Elliot gave free rein to the worst mood Kacie had ever seen him in.

'Shall I come back at two?' she asked when Mrs

Watts went out.

'Do you need a whole sixty minutes to eat? You were late getting here,' he reminded her unfairly. 'There's no room in my business for part-timers.'

'If I may say so, Mr Quantrell,' said Kacie, remembering the times she had worked so hard that she had not had a minute to catch her breath, 'you must be the worst patient ever known.'

'I'm not an invalid, Miss Peters,' he roared.

'So—I'll be back at one-thirty,' she told him.

After thirty minutes spent in thinking how life must be hell for Elliot at the moment, Kacie returned to the study determined to bear with him no matter how much he provoked her.

'Joe's been busy,' she said lightly, noticing at once that on an additional table over by the window, sat her typewriter.

Elliot too, she thought, as they resumed work, seemed to be making a conscious effort to control his frustration. For the next couple of hours they worked, if not in harmony, then without him throwing some unwarranted sarcastic offering her way.

With her back to him she began to type, but she did not get on very well. Without the ability to see to write, he would constantly interrupt her with some question or other.

It was nearing four when he halted her again to enquire about some matter she had dealt with in his absence the previous Thursday. Kacie stopped typing, and without turning around, explained the situation thus far, then went to make up time on her machine when suddenly she caught sight of thick snow flakes falling past the window.

'It's snowing!' she exclaimed.

Then she got the shock of her life to hear him state brusquely, 'I can *see* that!'

She spun round so fast she nearly fell off her chair. He had removed his dark glasses! Words rose rapidly— with no regard to sounding bossy—to tell him to put them on again, when she became side-tracked. Suddenly she had the feeling he had removed the darkened lenses some time ago, and had the most uncanny sensation that, since the effect of his eye drops must now have worn off, he had been watching her without her knowing it!

Plain common sense told her he would not waste his precious vision in contemplating her. She regained some vestige of prim composure.

'If you can see the snow, it must be time for your drops.' Her watch confirmed it was as close to four o'clock as made no difference. 'My hands are all carbon,' she said, getting to her feet, 'I'll go and wash them.'

She gave him a full ten minutes in which to use his eye dropper in private, but she was impatient to get back. She still had a mountain of typing to get through. If she could have thought of some tactful way to tell him she would much prefer to work without his constant interruptions, she might well have used it.

But no sooner had she returned to the study than her emotions were again thrown out of gear. Elliot was wearing his dark glasses once more, and her heart went out to him. Had that tactful phrase she had been seeking suddenly come to her then, Kacie knew she could never have used it. For although she knew he would never acknowledge it, she felt even if it was only to shoot her down, Elliot had need of that verbal contact.

Kacie began to get worried on her own behalf when at a quarter to five she took another glance to the window. There was a positive blizzard raging out there!

She remembered the narrow and apparently seldom used road which linked Ashwith Court with the outside world, and despaired. A minor road would not be gritted, that was certain. She had a vision of the terrible time she would have making her way along it before she came to any major road! She was conscious then that no matter if she did earn herself another remark about part-timers, that she had better start making noises about leaving before the rest of the threatening sky emptied its load.

'It's—snowing hard,' she volunteered as a tester.

'I'm thrilled,' came the sour reply to her back.

'I wasn't thinking of taking you sledging.' The acidic remark shot from her lips before she could stop it.

Oh God, she thought, and turned to look at him. It was nerves of course, which made her snap like that. Nerves brought on by the anticipation of his short, sharp and unpleasant response once she told him she thought she had better make tracks for home.

'I'm—sorry.' Reluctantly she apologised for her remark, though her observation of his unsmiling mouth did nothing to make her feel any better. 'It's just that if I don't leave now, then, if this snow keeps up, I'm going to have a devil of a job getting home.'

'Then,' said Elliot, on the look out for someone to fight with she was sure, 'you had better stay the night here.'

'Stay . . .!' Taken aback, Kacie was dumbstruck.

'Of course, if you've cleared your desk of work . . .' he suggested, as though hell-bent on needling her.

'I haven't finished,' she told him coldly, starting to get annoyed. Bored by his enforced inactivity, he seemed intent on brightening his bleak day by playing some game of cat and mouse with her.

'Then stay you must,' he pronounced silkily.

Kacie counted to ten, and added another three on account of the dreadful time he must be going through. Then she told him calmly.

'I can't stay.'

'Why not?' he bit, his silky tone giving way to aggression.

'Because . . .' She was not sure herself why she was making an issue of it. She had spent more than enough time pining for the sight of him, though she supposed a day spent in his tough and blunt company had brought a need to go home to lick her bruised feelings. 'Because, for one thing, I haven't a thing with me other than what I stand up in,' she said at last.

'Where's the problem?' he asked, and went on, 'While I don't own a set of pyjamas to lend you, I'm sure Mrs Watts can find you something guaranteed to cover your modesty. Unless,' he continued, his aggression unabated, 'you're determined to return to London because of some *heavy* date?'

'I've no date for tonight,' she told him woodenly. Then wondered how, when she loved him so much it was like a physical ache; when all her sympathy was his for his plight; she should at the same time feel the urge to box his ears.

'My God! You're slipping!' he snarled.

She stamped down the impulse to go over and hit him. 'What do I do for a toothbrush?'

'Mrs Watts probably has one tucked up her sleeve somewhere.'

Kacie ran out of arguments. Without another word, she turned back to her typewriter. She knew that, on hearing her type, Elliot had accepted she would not be returning to London that night. But even so, when at five-thirty he ordered her to have a cup of tea, and told her to instruct Mrs Watts to make a room ready for her, his acceptance of her decision to stay did not stop Kacie from going to the front door to take a quick look outside.

She saw the blizzard was still raging, indeed it seemed to be snowing harder than ever. One look at how the snow had settled on the drive was enough to convince her of how foolhardy it would be to try and make it back to her flat when her work was done.

She did not linger over her tea, but when she returned to the study, it was to find Elliot, either by himself, or with the help of Joe, had gone.

Kacie told herself she was glad. Now, she could get on with some work, But as she absorbed herself in her labour, she was all the while conscious that Elliot was not there.

By seven o'clock, she had made great inroads into her typing. One way and another, it had been a tiring day, so she was not at all sorry when Mrs Watts came with Elliot's instruction that she should stop work for the night.

'Mr Quantrell suggested you might like to see your room before dinner,' Mrs Watts told her pleasantly.

Kacie went with the housekeeper to a beautifully appointed bedroom, where Mrs Watts showed her a nightdress she had placed beneath the pillows, and asked her not to hesitate to ask if there was anything else she required.

'I'm sure you have supplied everything I need.' Kacie thanked her with a smile, and had her smile returned when the housekeeper told her dinner would be ready at eight, and then went on her way.

A trace of a smile curved Kacie's mouth again when she went into the adjoining bathroom to freshen up, and she saw that alongside a fresh tube of toothpaste, lay a cellophane wrapped toothbrush. Her thoughts went on to consider how with Elliot's eye drops due every four hours, at eight, his sight would again be gone. She knew beforehand, she would be dining alone.

In the dining-room an hour later, Kacie owned that she was again eager for sight of Elliot. A small sigh left her. She would not see him again before morning.

How could she have felt like physically setting about him when he had so much to contend with? He had been in a filthy mood for most of the day, but when he normally had so much energy that he made everyone else around seem stationary, was it any wonder he was short on patience? It must have been utterly intolerable, when he usually read and comprehended at great speed, to have to sit and listen while she stumbled her way through complicated technical reports.

Kacie finished her meal, and left the dining-room vowing that no matter how much Elliot tried her temper tomorrow, she was not going to let him get to her. She would not rise to his baiting, no matter how sarcastic or vile he was, she promised herself as she went along the hall.

When she went to pass a door which had been left wide open, she suddenly caught sight of him sitting with a glass of Scotch in his hand. Her heart beat a familiar up-tempo beat just to see him, and she hesitated.

'Who's there?' he asked sharply, his ears obviously well attuned to all sound.

'It's me . . . Kacie,' she said, and went forward into the drawing-room.

Elliot seemed to neither want her presence or her company, for he had no comment to make. She felt foolish and tried to think up something fairly intelligent to say.

'I've just finished dinner,' was the best she could manage. 'I was just thinking of turning in,' she added when he did not appear to find her first comment all that scintillating. 'Mrs Watts found me a toothbrush,' she went on, then realised she was babbling with nervousness. 'Well then . . . Good night, Elliot,' she said, and nearly died when his first name just slipped out.

His reply was to raise his Scotch glass to his lips as if toasting not having to hear her until morning. Kacie moved over to the door, and was through it and on her way to closing it when the realisation struck that the door had been left open on purpose to give him clear passage.

She went back into the room to make sure the door was left wide and would stay wide. As she did so she could not resist looking over to where he sat. Seeing him looking so alone, so inactive, she had to ask, 'Is there anything I can do for you before I . . .'

'What have you in mind?' His voice, harsh, unfriendly, and with barely disguised sarcasm, sliced her off.

'Nothing especially,' she replied quietly. 'I just thought that before I went to bed . . .'

'For God's sake, go to bed and leave me in peace,' he grated. 'I'm not remotely interested in having you play nursemaid.'

'I wasn't . . .' she tried to deny hotly, her resolve not to get angry with him sorely under attack.

'Nor, if you have some idea of tucking me up in bed out of harm's way,' he butted in, 'am I remotely interested in giving you the cheap thrill of undressing me.'

'Undressing you!' Kacie exploded. Several times that day her temper had come near to fraying, but at his sudden and unjust accusation, her sorely tried temper frayed. 'Whatever you're dressed in, you're a swine,' she erupted, 'so I can't imagine the mere removal of your clothing would bring about a personality change. But,' she hurried on furiously, 'far from wanting a thrill—cheap or otherwise—you can damn well sleep and rot in your clothes, for all I care.'

She was still hating Elliot Quantrell as she charged up to her room and got ready for bed, then went to wash her underwear and hang it to dry overnight.

But by the time she eventually climbed into bed, she was regretting her volatile response to his remarks. Oh confound it, she sighed, so much for all her promise to take everything he threw at her, with equanimity! It was not tomorrow yet, and already she had broken her vow not to let him get to her!

CHAPTER SEVEN

On waking the next morning, Kacie was immediately conscience-stricken to remember how she had allowed Elliot to goad her into losing her temper. Her conscience dug away at her as she bathed and dressed. She thought of the terrible time he was living through, and could not wait to leave her room to make amends.

As if to oustrip her thoughts, she raced down to breakfast. She was resolved. No matter how much he needled away at her, no matter what insulting or sarcastic comment he thought up to goad her with, she would not lose her temper.

Accordingly, no sooner had Kacie finished the bacon and eggs Mrs Watts plied her with, than she was making her way to the study where she knew Elliot would be waiting.

Any notion that he might have completed his course of treatment was not borne out when she saw that he still wore his dark lenses. Determined to be bright and breezy, even if it killed her, she put behind all sad thoughts of how he must be feeling about the fact that the four hourly eye drop insertions were not yet over.

'Good morning,' she said cheerfully, and walked over to her typewriter. In response he opened the day with a sour; 'What happened to the bad tempered bitch who didn't wait for me to wish her a good night?'

There it was again, that needling note! Kacie remembered her resolve.

'It's your charm that does it,' she replied sunnily,

and discovered she had squashed any comeback, when the only rejoinder he made was a snort of sound which could have been repressed amusement, but, in the circumstance of his sour mood, was more probably a snort of disgust.

Anything was better than his heavily loaded sarcasm. She had come close, she admitted, to telling him it had been his diabolical mood and his bad tempered words which had seen her hasten away without giving him the chance to say good night. Not that she believed anything else he had to say to her last night would have been anything as mild as a civil farewell.

Kacie continued with her typing from where she had left off. But ten minutes later she had confirmation that Elliot had inserted his eye drops that morning, when he broke into her concentration to ask her for a telephone number.

She turned in her seat, and saw the telephone index there on the desk before him. Her sympathy was such then, that only a sensitivity to his sense of independence prevented her from going to press out the digits for him.

Over the next hour he interrupted her many times to ask for a number. But she was glad she had restrained herself, for, given a few faulty digits, he was getting on famously.

What was more, as he progressed, so the grim note went from his voice. No one, she was certain, would ever know that there was anything wrong with him. Not once did he say he was calling from home, and as far as any of the people he rang knew, he was phoning from his office.

Another plus was that he even forgot to be uncivil with her. His last call had started to sound more than a little involved and she automatically reached for her note pad. As he put the phone down, he asked, 'Did you get that?'

'Every word,' she replied, and was really uplifted, when, as if it had only just dawned on him he had not asked her to make a note of any of the quoted figures he had repeated back to the other person, he graciously thanked her.

At midday she left the study tactfully to allow him to insert his eye drops. She had nearly run out of work by then, and knew it would only be a matter of time before she returned to an office where work went on non-stop. With her journey back to London in mind, she took a look outside to see that although snow lay deep, it was no longer raging a blizzard.

She was of the belief as she returned to the study, that, provided she took it steadily, and provided she went in daylight, she should reach the office that afternoon without mishap.

'That's about everything I've brought with me,' she told Elliot after about fifteen minutes of sorting through the remainder of her papers. 'I'll start loading these files into my car. The . . .'

'You're thinking of going somewhere?'

She swallowed a sigh that it had not taken him long to lose his civil tone. 'I'm through here, wouldn't you say?' she asked, and not waiting for his reply, 'There are loads of things I can be doing at the office. If I go now . . .'

'You're going nowhere,' he sliced her off sharply.

'Why not?' she asked, rising to his sudden sharp tone before she could remember her resolve.

He had that look about him, she observed, which said he was about to reply bluntly 'Because I say so.' But, although it amounted to much the same, what he actually said, was, 'Because you can't get out.'

'I'm sure I can,' she replied, although his statement

had immediately knocked a dent in her confidence. 'It had stopped snowing when I took a look outside just now, and although it was a bit drifty in places, I'm sure if I . . .'

'Did you take a look at the road at the end of the drive?'

'No, but . . .'

'It's blocked,' he said shortly, his tone indicating that the subject was closed.

'How . . .' Her sensitivity had her unable to complete the sentence. Elliot hated his blindness, without her ramming home a reminder of it.

'How do I know?' He had no such qualms about finishing for her. Kacie stayed silent, but felt no less miserable and uncomfortable, when he went on, 'I may be temporarily without the ability to assess the conditions personally, but impaired vision has not taken from me the everyday ability to talk to a stranded milkman.'

While she had still been in bed, Elliot, restless and frustrated, had been downstairs early when the milkman had arrived. Kacie felt wretched and thought she should say something.

'The sun's come out now,' she said gently. 'Perhaps the roads are better now than they were earlier on.'

'They're not.' He flattened the idea—and flattened her too, when he added, 'Joe will tell me the moment it's possible for you to get your car out.'

Love for Elliot made her pride a tender and an easily bruised creature where he was concerned. But his unveiled hint that he was eager for her to go and could not wait to have Joe's report, had her positive he could not be half as eager for her to be on her way as she was.

'What did the stranded milkman do?' she asked, belligerently.

'How the hell should I know?' he questioned

toughly, his temper showing signs of being ragged.
'Once he'd made use of the telephone, he was off.'

'Lucky him!' Kacie snapped. 'I'll bet he manages
to get to his own bed tonight!'

'Resign yourself to the fact you're bedding down at
Ashwith for another night.' Elliot exploded. 'Is it so
very dreadful here, that you . . .?' Suddenly, he stilled.
Whatever thought had just come to him, she knew she
was not going to like it. Neither did she, when he
snarled, 'I've got it wrong haven't I? The only reason
you're straining at the leash to get back to town tonight,
is not because you want your own bed, but because
you have a date in the bed of one of your many . . .'

'Don't you *dare* say it,' Kacie yelled.

'Why shouldn't I,' he challenged grittily, 'if it's the
truth?'

How she prevented herself from hitting him then,
she did not know. Her hand *itched* to strike him.
Regardless of his dark glasses, she *wanted* to slap
him—hard. But she would never forgive herself
afterwards if she could not control the violent feelings
he had provoked. Kacie dared not stay in the room
with him a minute longer.

'Go to hell, Elliot,' she said quietly, and even
though there were still twenty-five minutes to go
before lunch, she walked out of the study.

She had nowhere near got herself together when her
watch showed one. But pride wouldn't let her show
Mrs Watts that she was upset, and she went to the
dining-room although she was not in the least hungry.

When Kacie had finished picking at her lunch she
went up to her room, and stayed there to go over and
over again what she saw as Elliot's low opinion of her.
She was glad then that she had told him to go to hell.
No man, she thought had a right to speak to her that
way, be he friend, enemy, or employer.

It hurt that he should think her ready to jump into bed with every man she came into contact with. It was that hurt, she realised, which had seen her fighting hard not to physically lash out at him.

Half past one, the time she had returned to the study yesterday, had long since gone. Two o'clock came and went, and Kacie made no move to leave her room. Every time she softened for long enough to consider she had better go and see if Elliot had found something for her to do, her acquiescent soul would mutiny and she would find herself thinking; why should I?

If he wants me, let him send for me, she thought on a flurry of indignation. But as the hands of her watch neared three, and no such summons came, she was ashamed that in her hurt she had lost sight of the unbearable time he was going through just now.

Kacie left her room, and made for the study. Without bothering to knock she opened the door and went in. Then any last remnants of rebellion disappeared without trace. Remorse sent them fleeing. Elliot, she saw, with not a scrap of his beloved work in front of him, was wearing an expression which told her how utterly fed up he was to have to sit twiddling his thumbs.

'It occurred to me,' she said, her voice level, cool even, 'you might need a few phone numbers.'

'So good of you to condescend to remember you have a job,' he drawled.

So there was to be no let up in hostilities. 'Think nothing of it,' she replied, the sarcasm in her coming out for an airing. 'It's a joy to work with you, Mr Quantrell,' she murmured—it was either that, or let him trample all over her.

She fully expected to have him fire back, with both barrels.

To her immense astonishment, however, a hint of a

curve suddenly came to his well shaped mouth, and he asked, 'Am I really such a swine?'

Her heart was all at once on a merry-go-round; her breath caught. After hours and hours of him being all of the swine she had twice called him, to see that charm, that hint of humour, was a shock. A wonderful, beautiful shock. She was about to tell him she did not think him a swine at all. But just in time, she realised that any such words might well give him the impression that she was eager to forgive him anything. Hurriedly she found something else to say.

'Have you been outside the house, at all, since you came home last Saturday?' she asked, suddenly inspired by an idea.

'Where would I go—without a ball of string?' he replied, albeit less grimly.

'I'll be your ball of string, if you like,' she hurried to volunteer. To save his pride she added quickly, 'I've barely had any exercise this two days. I could do with a walk.'

His face went expressionless, and she braced herself for some sarcastic comment on what he considered her usual form of exercise. She told herself she would get angry when he made it known he did not think that a walk outside might do him some good.

But to her surprise, his only comment was a dry, 'Spare me from fit badminton types, who think nothing of tramping about in snow drifts.'

'Oh!' she exclaimed. 'I'd forgotten the snow!'

'You surprise me,' he murmured, in oblique reference to how the spat they'd had before lunch had begun all on account of the snow.

'I meant,' Kacie evaded, feeling a shade uncomfortable at the reminder that she had taken a lunch break of over two hours, 'that I'd forgotten that any glare coming off the snow, might affect your eyes.'

'I doubt anything will get through these lenses,' he replied. In his usual manner he had everything cut and dried, his decision made, when he said, 'All right. I've some gum boots in the back cloakroom. We'll go and see if Mrs Watts can tog you out in similar fashion.'

A song started somewhere inside Kacie, but even so, anxiety about the snow affecting his eyes made her ask:

'You're sure? About your eyes? I mean, has the doctor warned you . . .'

'Believe me, Kacie, since the accident I've discovered just how very much I value my sight. No matter how irksome I find it to obey orders, there's no way I am going to do anything which might prevent a full recovery.'

'Oh!' she exclaimed again. Then, whether he saw her concern for him or not, she just had to ask, 'But— you've made arrangements to see an opthalmologist?'

'What a fusspot you are,' said Elliot, and her heart beat a rapid tattoo again when she saw a definite curve to his mouth. 'Should he be able to get through, I've a consultant paying a visit tomorrow. Now, unless you have plans to be regaled with the rest of my medical history, slight though it is, can we go?'

'Yes, sir,' she said meekly, and felt her spirit ascend into the clouds when she heard him laugh.

What she looked like in Mrs Watts' oversized wellingtons and anorak, Kacie did not care to know. But Elliot could not see her, and all was right with her world.

'A pathway's been cleared,' she told him when, with his hand on her arm, she led him out of the back door. 'Joe?' she asked.

'Joe,' he confirmed.

A short while later they rounded the side of the house. 'It's beautiful out here!' she exclaimed. Then mindful as they started to descend the long drive that he could not see, she began to describe the snow laden boughs and the distant hedgerows which lay under a blanket of white.

Kacie was never more careful of where she was placing her feet as they strolled, and she watched where Elliot was placing his. But in between the moments when she was busy watching where she was guiding him, she would look up to describe more of the scene.

Alert to the need to keep him clear of the frequent snow banks, she progressed steadily with him to the end of the drive. When, in the process of guiding him around the biggest snow drift they had so far come across, Kacie took a moment to glance up, about, and beyond, she stopped dead suddenly. The road beyond the drive was clear!

She came to an abrupt halt, exclaiming in surprise. As she jerked against Elliot, he moved towards the snow drift and her too-fast remedial action was to result in them both falling over into the drift.

'Are you all right?' she gasped hurriedly, winded by his weight on top of her. Panic grabbed her when he did not reply, and her urgent fingers went to lift his face from where it was tucked into the side of her neck.

'You smell good,' he murmured, raising his head at the feel of her hands on his skin.

Relief surged through her, but his comment had reminded her how important, in the absence of his sight, his sense of smell and other faculties must be to him.

'Are you hurt?' she asked, more relief flooding her to see that somehow his dark glasses had stayed with him.

'Of the two of us,' said Elliot, his voice totally devoid of abrasion, 'I'd say I had the softer landing.'

'You're—all right—though?' she asked, feeling shaky at the sudden realisation that instinctively, protectively perhaps, Elliot had snatched her into his arms as they had gone down, and that he still had his arms around her.

'How about you?' he countered, and there was a quality in his voice that she had never heard before.

'I'm—f-fine,' she stammered.

She felt his arms tighten about her. Her heart was beating like a trip hammer as he looked down into her face with unseeing eyes. All at once she felt such a tremendous tension in him, that it transmitted itself to her.

'C-can—you see?' she asked jerkily, and then, afraid of what *her* eyes might be revealing, she closed them.

Something whispered down to her lips. She wanted it to be his mouth, and kept her eyes closed. But whether Elliot had just kissed her, whether he had merely brushed a snowflake from her mouth, or whether she had just imagined the whole of it, Kacie did not discover.

Abruptly he pulled away from her. 'The extent of my vision is such,' he answered her, 'that it must be time for more drops.'

By the time they were both on their feet, she was more concerned that, whatever the extent of his vision, Elliot should not take another fall in the snow. He stood as though striving to get his bearings while she brushed the heaviest snow from him.

With some urgency, he suddenly said, 'We'll go back to the house.'

Tactfully she turned him about to face the way they should go, and glanced at her watch to see they should be back well in time for him to administer his four o'clock drops.

He was as silent on the return as he had been when

they set off. Kacie relived that feeling of tension that had started with him, but which had rapidly taken a hold of her. She was at a loss as to what to make of it.

'We're stepping on to the section Joe cleared,' she thought to tell him when they neared the house. Then memory of what she had been about to tell him before they had fallen over suddenly returned. 'Which reminds me,' she went on, 'the road at the bottom of the dr . . .'

'I wonder what Mrs Watts is cooking for our dinner,' Elliot interrupted, his voice so pleasant, so affable, that Kacie momentarily lost track again.

'You're hungry?' she enquired.

'Starving,' he admitted, to make her wonder if, since his accident, impatient with himself and his lack of ability to know what was on his plate, he had preferred not to eat at all.'

'Perhaps,' she suggested; loving him in this more friendly mood with every ounce of her being, 'Mrs Watts would bring dinner forward a little?'

'Perhaps ,' he replied, 'you would dine with me this evening, Miss Peters?'

'I'd be delighted, Mr Quantrell,' she told him.

They went into the kitchen where Elliot instructed Mrs Watts they would like to dine at seven-thirty, and Kacie, divested of anorak and wellingtons, sailed up to her room with her eyes all of a sparkle. At eight, Elliot would insert his drops, but for the half hour up until then, he would be able to see well enough to eat his dinner without breaking off half way through in frustrated impatience.

Before Kacie was due to go down to dinner, however, the basic honesty in her soul had reared its head. The result of which was for her to have one enormous inner argument. Recalling that the snow plough had been along the road at the bottom of the

drive, she knew no reason why she should stay to
dinner, or, for that matter, why she should stay the
night either.

Honesty decreed she should go straight away to tell
him the road had been cleared. But that honesty was
bombarded by the memory of the happiness she had
known when another, friendlier side of Elliot had
shown through.

She needed to have more! She wanted to savour the
sound of his laugh again. She wanted to try and tease
that reluctant smile from him. Even though she had no
guarantee he would not return to being the brusque
surly brute she knew better, Kacie found she could not
leave. She was in love with him and so wanted the
chance of a few more hours of seeing this different
Elliot away from the office. There was no doubt in her
mind that when he returned to the office, he would
return to being the short-tempered, efficient employer,
who barked out his orders from nine to five.

Aware that Elliot would leave her at eight to
administer his drops, Kacie arrived in the dining-room
on the dot of half past seven, to find him already there.

'Sorry if I've kept you waiting,' she apologised, and
her heart gave a crazy flutter when he stood
courteously, and only resumed his seat when she had
taken her place at the table.

The magic of his charm gripped her as he showed
that he was still the same man she had parted from in
the kitchen. The perfect host, he engaged her in light
conversation. And so enamoured of him was she that
she ate whatever Mrs Watts served, but had no
recollection afterwards of what the dish had been.

They were on the second course when he asked her
if her family lived in London. Kacie's heart gave
another flutter that, even though he was just being
polite—and that was a rare enough occurrence where

she was concerned—he was showing an interest in her as a person, and not as a piece of office machinery.

'My mother lives near Stratford-on-Avon with my stepfather,' she willingly told him.

'Your parents are divorced?' he queried.

'My father died when I was small,' she explained, and saw no reason not to tell him, 'My stepfather is the dearest man. I was never more pleased when my mother agreed to marry him.' She might then have gone on to tell him of the sacrifices her mother had made for her, but out of the blue, with a sudden edge to his voice, Elliot asked her:

'You've never been married?'

'Good heavens, no!' she exclaimed. She knew for a fact he had been through her personnel file with a magnifying glass, and would have instant recall of every full stop and comma. 'Why do you ask?' she questioned, caution making her tone sharp. She was wary at the sudden notion that he must think she had made a false statement about her spinsterhood, and was maybe trying to trip her up.

'The question was a natural enough one,' he replied. 'Your beauty draws many admirers to you—some of whom have doubtless asked you to marry them. But since you aren't married, and tell me you never have been, I can only assume that either you're more interested in your career, or that the right man hasn't asked you yet.'

She had a sudden vivid recollection of how, at their first meeting, he had discounted any suggestion that she was career-minded. While not wanting a discussion on that subject, however, neither did she want to be drawn on the subject of 'the right man'. Quickly she turned the conversation back on him.

'Have you ever been married?' she asked.

His charm was again in evidence when, the corners

of his mouth picking up, he told her, 'I've seen too many marriages founder to view the concept of matrimony with anything but a jaundiced eye.'

'Cynic,' she tossed at him lightly, and was almost faint with joy when she heard him briefly laugh. She wanted to know if Lana Neasom was a divorcée, but Kacie saw that with this talk of marriage and the right person for it, she might find herself landed in a mine-field of her own making if she did not take care.

Mrs Watts saved the day, by arriving to exchange their dinner plates for pudding dishes. Kacie searched for a topic which had not the slightest connection with marriage, or more exactly, the people one fell in love with. But the only other subject matter to pop into her head was the guilty conscience-stricken memory of how the road at the bottom of the drive had been cleared. So when Mrs Watts departed, Kacie launched into matters she had not wanted to talk of either—office matters.

Whether the subject entertained him, she could not tell. But Elliot voiced no objection to going along with her.

When, however, in connection with some programme Cecil Glover's name cropped up, Kacie, on a sudden impulse asked, 'He reported me, didn't he?'

Instantly, she wished she had not asked. As chairman of the company, Elliot was bound to take more note of what a director told him, in preference to what his secretary might say. She had spoiled it all and thought she had just dispelled any friendliness Elliot had shown her, when suddenly she was taken aback to see that although there was not a hint of a smile on his face—neither was he scowling!

'Yes, he did report you,' he solemnly confirmed.

'But—but you didn't—er—tell me . . . I mean ask me, about it.'

'Make no mistake, Kacie,' Elliot told her evenly, 'Cecil Glover is damned good at his job. But even though I've known and worked with him for a number of years, and appreciate his genius in his field, that doesn't mean that I'm ignorant of certain flaws in his character, which I admire less.' Then Elliot smiled and murmured, in a conspiratorial way that made her heart skip, 'I admire much more a fiery young redhead who had enough pluck to tell him to keep his hands to himself.'

Elliot had not thought it necessary to question her over the affair, or to take her to task because she had offended one of his directors. Emotion threatened to choke her. She then feared that any reply she made might, in her emotional gratitude, reveal more than gratitude ... perhaps even betray the depth of her love.

She took her eyes from him, and suddenly felt a need to be alone while she got herself together again. Afraid to look at him again, but needing to look somewhere, she glanced at her watch. At first the time did not register, but suddenly, it did.

Quickly she was on her feet, hoping that he would think she was merely being tactful and that she had no reason to leave other than to afford him privacy to insert his drops, 'It's way past eight,' she told him, and went swiftly from the dining-room.

She was still floating on air an hour later. Elliot admired her, he had said so! Well, her basic honesty had to qualify, he admired her pluck in telling Cecil Glover what she had anyway.

But nothing would dampen the glow she felt to know Elliot admired *something* about her! As happy as she felt just then, she resisted the strong impulse to return downstairs and join him.

By now his vision would be gone, which, if all she

had heard was accurate, meant he would have a greater perception through his other faculties. Fear that he might sense her elation—ever a man to seek to find a cause, no matter how obscure—kept Kacie in her room.

She decided she had better undress and get into bed. That way, should the impulse to go to him try to get the better of her again, by the time she was up and dressed, the strength of it should have weakened.

Kacie took off her shoes and tights, then unbuttoned the cuffs of her shirt. She had started on the buttons down the front of her shirt, when the most horrendous crash came from the room next door.

Elliot! Alarm and fear for him ousted every thought in her head. She was not thinking; capable only of instinctive feeling, when like lightning she bolted from her room. Elliot was in trouble was all she knew and in response, she shot like a rocket into the next door room.

She breathed again when she saw Elliot, with not a mark on him, look up from where he was stooped over by an antique desk.

'I'll help,' she said, drawing another relieved breath as she went forward to assist him in picking up a heavy, solid brass table lamp, an assortment of weighty tomes, and various papers which had all been sent flying.

'It would appear I set off a domino effect when, in an absent-minded moment, I reached out to switch the lamp on,' he murmured.

Kacie took the lamp from his hands, her heartbeats settling down now that she knew he was safe. 'Nothing's broken, though I expect your bulb's done for,' she said, her cheerful tone hiding her concern at the fact that, obviously needing some light in his darkness, Elliot had discarded his dark glasses.

She bent to help him pick up another couple of books, telling herself not to be the fusspot he had called her. The only light in the room came from a shaded lamp over by the bed, and could in no way be called glaring. Besides which, he must be sick to death of those dark glasses.

Kacie placed the last of the books in its position on the desk, but was loath to go back to her room in case he had not yet got his bearings. She hesitated, and thought how dear to her he was, and seconds passed with Elliot just standing as though looking at her. I love you, my darling, she thought, but you will never know it.

Afraid then to bring out some breezy good night, lest her voice came out all emotional, she half turned, intending to leave. But as she moved, Elliot stretched his hands out to her, and all her love rose up as she reaslised that, disorientated and unable to see where he was going, Elliot, dear proud Elliot, was silently asking her to give him some direction.

She turned to him, her arms stretching out. Their fingers touched, clasped, and then Kacie was gripping on to his hands as tightly he held hers.

'Kacie,' he said softly, and whether he was thanking her for understanding, or whatever he meant, she could no more hold back from calling his name, than she could fly.

'Elliot,' she said, her voice a whisper, and in the next moment, as though it was meant to be, she was in his arms.

To feel his mouth warm over hers was to end a day that had started out so grimly, with perfect conclusion. But it did not end there. For if one kiss was not enough for her, Kacie rejoiced that one kiss was not enough for him either.

Again and again he kissed her, his arms strong about

her, his hands warm and caressing at her back. 'Elliot,' she breathed again, and his mouth returned to tease her lips apart.

She felt his hands warm through the thinness of her shirt, and the feel of him, his hard muscled body so close, lit a fire inside her such as she had never known.

Lost to everything save him, she wanted to be closer to him. When Elliot pulled her hard up against him, she in turn, with her arms wrapped around him, pressed herself to him.

Who guided whom towards the bed, she could not have said, but she went willingly. Beside the bed they stood, excitement and passion overwhelming and commanding of every part of her when, with his left arm holding her, the fingers of his right hand undid the buttons of her shirt.

When he took her shirt from her and gathered her to him, she felt not the smallest embarrassment, but gloried to feel his mobile lips as he traced kisses down over her throat, and to the swell of her breasts before returning to claim her mouth.

She felt his hands at the waistband of her skirt, and knew an urgency to help him relieve her of the garment. But his expert fingers needed no assistance. For suddenly, although she had felt not the smallest tug of movement, her skirt lay on the floor.

Clad in only her briefs and bra, her heart raced. A fever of wanting took her as Elliot pressed her to him and showed the same need of her which she had for him.

That desire became almost too great to be borne as she felt his hands on the naked skin of her back. She wanted to cry out a command, a plea, for him to take possession of her but the words were lost under the gamut of pleasurable emotions that rioted through her as he undid the clasp of her bra.

She could find no words to describe her ecstasy as

Elliot removed her bra, and moved his warm caressing hands gently over her breasts. Her hands clutched desperately at him, and her head went back to allow him all the freedom he wanted to move his mouth over her. A sigh of rapture left her parted lips.

'Elliot,' she moaned his name.

'Adorable Kacie,' he murmured, and without being conscious of how she had got there, or when he had removed his shirt, she found she was on his bed with him.

'Kiss me,' she pleaded. Her need for him had become a craving.

Elliot kissed her, this time a kiss which plundered her mouth, and brought from her such a response that he pulled back and, just as if he could see her, a warm curve appeared on his mouth.

'Your fire matches mine, sweet love,' he told her throatily. Kacie felt herself in heaven to hear him call her 'sweet love', while his sightless eyes travelled the length of her body. 'You're beautiful, Kacie,' he breathed tenderly. 'I thought your face beautiful, but your body, is a delight.'

For all of two seconds more, she lay and luxuriated in another world while he looked down at her, and at the body he thought was a delight. Then suddenly, every one of her inhibitions which up until that point had been abandoned in her desire suddenly sprang out of hiding.

Instinctively she retrieved her hands to cover her breasts. Her voice hoarse, she croaked, 'Y-you—c-can—see me?'

A frown of puzzlement came to his brow at her action. 'Yes,' he confirmed, 'I can see you.'

On the instant, scarlet colour scorched her face. Neither shyness nor embarrassment had intruded upon her pleasure, but suddenly, she was swamped by both.

It was that embarrassment; that shyness; the sudden realisation of being near-naked before a man for the first time in her life; that made the fire he had aroused dim. In a whirlpool of mixed emotions, she pulled away from him. Her movement took her to the side of the bed, when with not even the vaguest awareness of what she was doing, instinct had her grabbing up her shirt to hold it in front of her.

'Y-your—eye drops?' she questioned faintly, her underlying concern for him taking over.

'Eye drops?' he echoed. His astonishment at this turn of events was all too obvious as he too left the bed. A harsh note sharpened his voice as he told her, 'I finished the course of eye drops at four this afternoon.'

Although she was not really conscious of where she was any more, as the revelation sank in, what Kacie could discern, was that his mood had changed.

Elliot, ever a proud man, had worked it all out, and all at once he was blisteringly angry. In no time at all, in a voice which could have brought down tower blocks, he was shattering her ear drums with his fury.

'*Kacie!*' he roared. '*Pity!* You'd have let me make love to you out of *pity!*'

'No!' she denied, not enough together yet to realise it might be better if she had said 'yes'.

'Damn your impudence!' he bellowed, and moved towards her. Nervously, Kacie backed away, only to find that he had moved merely to pick up the remainder of her clothing. 'Take these,' he thundered, thrusting her bra and her skirt at her, 'and yourself, out of my sight.'

His rage as he went striding to the door and pulled it wide, was such as Kacie had never seen. Totally stunned, she went to the door, but Elliot had not finished yet. More harsh words rained down on her head.

'Remember in future,' he snarled, 'that any "favours" I might want, I can get without having to use the subterfuge of blindness to lure a woman to my bed.'

Kacie was through the door when her numbed emotion started to reawaken. She felt pain and hurt. Before she could open her mouth, however—though what she would have uttered, she knew not—he had beaten her to it.

'You might also remember,' he told her with harsh insolence, 'that I have no intention whatever, of paying for anything other than your secretarial services.'

Cut to the quick by his invective, her jaw dropped. In the next moment, though, she was overwhelmed by a wave of uncontrollable anger.

'Why you . . .' she started to retaliate. It was as far as she got. By the simple expedient of slamming his bedroom door shut in her face, Elliot silenced her.

CHAPTER EIGHT

THE man who had haunted her thoughts throughout a sleepless night, haunted them still when at first light Kacie started out for London. The decision to leave Ashwith Court had been made for her when Elliot had thrown her out of his room and slammed the door in her face. How she had hated him then!

Just as he hated her, she supposed, in his belief that she had given herself to him out of pity. Pity had nothing to do with her reaction to him from the moment of that first kiss. But by then Kacie had seen that to have him believe what he did was her only salvation. Pride demanded that he should never know how she felt about him.

Would a woman who pitied him to the extent that he believed her to just disappear from his home without a word?

Pride resolved that issue too. No woman with anything about her, she concluded, would stand for getting unceremoniously ejected from a man's room, and be ready the next time she saw him to behave as though nothing had happened. Not so soon anyway.

Kacie was nearly at her flat when, her mind so full of Elliot, it occurred to her to think of the mass of files and the typewriter she had taken with her to Ashwith Court. Her next thought was that perhaps this was it! Perhaps now was the time she should not only part company with Elliot, but with Quantrell Industries altogether.

Inside her flat she bathed, then found, when every scrap of her common sense decreed she should not go to the office that day—or ever again—that she had donned an office outfit.

Love for Elliot presented her with plenty of excuses to ignore common sense. For one thing, work was bound to be piling up. For another, even if the consultant's report today was favourable, Elliot would surely still have to rest his eyes for a while.

She did not expect to see him in the office today. Nor, when she recalled how she had stood before him near-naked—and all that had followed—was she ready to see him yet.

She did not see him that day, but she did hear from him. She arrived late for work, then chased up a spare typewriter. Fifteen minutes later she was hard at it, when Elliot phoned.

Kacie knew the way it was going to be from the moment she said, 'Mr Quantrell's secretary,' and heard his curt and icy voice interrupt her greeting.

'Anything in the post I should know about?' His tone was thick with hostility.

With difficulty, she managed to match that impersonal quality and relayed details of the mail, and if her insides felt like jelly, she was determined that only she should know of it. No sooner had she completed her résumé, than abruptly, he rang off.

That morning was the most unhappy one of her life. She took herself off to lunch still unable to be rid of her low spirits. She returned to find that during her absence someone had delivered not only her typewriter, but also every one of the files she had left at Ashwith Court.

Straight away she jumped to the conclusion that Elliot had received a good report about his eyes, and must be somewhere around in the building. Still nowhere near ready to face him, Kacie was immediately an agitated mass of nerves.

But when two-thirty had passed, and then three, with still no sign of him, she just had to set her nerves at rest, and rang reception to enquire if they knew anything about the returned files. She held on while the receptionist checked around, and then was relieved to find that even in one's darkest hours, there was a light, for the girl came back to tell her that the files had been returned by Joe. Kacie collapsed into weak giggles as her tension released.

Neither on Thursday, nor on Friday did Elliot put in an appearance, and her spirits sunk lower than ever. Her concern was all for him, and by the time Saturday arrived, she had worked herself up into a fine state.

'Is there anything wrong dear?' her mother asked when she rang.

'Nothing at all,' Kacie lied, wanting desperately to confide her fears for Elliot's sight, but unable to say a word.

'Are you sure? Your voice sounds all flat, and not like you at all.'

'I'm fine, honestly, I am,' Kacie replied, and did her best to inject a cheerful note throughout the rest of their conversation.

The bright manner she adopted fell away once their call ended, however, and she was back to praying with all her might that there was no permanent damage to Elliot's sight.

When she went to the office on Monday, he was at his desk, the dark glasses gone. Her joy almost had her beaming with an ear to ear grin. But his expression when he looked up, was not one of welcome.

'Good morning.' She swallowed her grin to greet him coolly.

'Good morning,' he replied brusquely.

So, in the first hour of his return, Kacie had an

endorsement of the way the coming week was going to be—impersonal.

Indeed, so impersonal was he, that many times during the week she was to wonder—had she really ever lain and been enchanted by the ardour of this automaton? For never, by word, look or deed, was there anything in his manner to suggest he had any memory that he had once desired her.

True she had glanced up once or twice and found his eyes on her. But his chilling expression when he saw himself observed was to tell her plainly that whatever he felt for her, it was certainly not desire.

She got on with her work, conscious all the time that he was still outraged and offended that she had dared to pity him. She wanted to know what the consultant had said about his eyes, but the solid barrier of ice between them prevented her from asking—she had offended him once on the subject, and knew it was now taboo.

By Friday afternoon, with both her physical and mental energy worn, Kacie could not doubt that the consultant's report had been a good one. If nothing else, the way Elliot had worked her and himself, this week, was living proof that the problem with his eyes must have cleared.

She was just thinking that of the two of them she would be the one going home with eye strain, when he returned from a meeting. Without a glance to her, he instructed curtly that she should bring the papers she had been working on through to his office. Papers in hand, her face composed, Kacie had just got to her feet, when the phone rang.

'Take that first,' barked Elliot through the open doorway.

Kacie put her papers down, picked up the phone, and said her usual piece. Then, with surprise, and a touch of anxiety, she heard the voice of her stepfather, who usually left the telephoning to her mother.

'William!' she exclaimed, afraid that something had happened to her mother.

'Your mother's out having her hair done,' he said to put some of her fears at rest.

'Something's wrong?' she quickly questioned.

'Not with us, we're as happy as the proverbial turtle doves,' he assured her. 'The thing is though, Kacie, your mother's been fretting all this week with some idea that you're not happy.'

'But I'm . . .'

'Which is why,' William butted in when she had been about to tell him she was just fine, 'I was sure if I had a quiet word, you might be able to find time to come down to see us.'

She had not paid a visit to Wellsingham since Christmas, and the guilt that afflicted her at that thought stirred Kacie to enthusiam. 'Of course, I can,' she told him, her voice overly cheerful.

'Lovely,' said William, and suggested, 'You'll stay the weekend. Your mother would like that—and so would I, of course.'

Sounds of Elliot's increasingly apparent impatience made Kacie rapidly aware that he was waiting for her paper work. 'There's nothing I'd like better than to spend the weekend with you . . .' Her voice broke off, the end of her acceptance of the invitation suddenly interrupted.

For Elliot, an absolutely furious Elliot, was striding to her desk. Obviously in no mind to hang about while she dallied taking personal calls, he snatched up the papers he had tired of waiting for, and gave her a withering hostile look before slamming back into his own office.

Oh grief, Kacie thought, not looking forward at all

to going in to see him. The phone was still in her hand reminding her that William was still on the other end. 'I'll be with you tomorrow,' she told him, and ended the call.

She had seen Elliot in some foul moods, but the one he was in when she went into his office topped the lot, Kacie thought.

She drove down to Wellsingham on Saturday, and had so much welcome and love showered on her, that by Monday she was again ready to cope with Elliot whatever mood he might be in—or so she thought.

Storm warnings were hoisted from the moment he ignored her cool greeting and without giving her time to stow her handbag away, began to give his orders.

By Wednesday, Kacie was beginning to wonder how on earth she put up with him. Two seconds later, she knew exactly why. For, filthy tempered swine though he had been just lately—not that she could ever remember him being angelic—she loved the brute.

In her conversation at the weekend, she had included snippets of her working day. She had found then that once having allayed her mother's fear of her being unhappy, her parent began to show concern on another front.

'I was a little worried after my last telephone call to you, Kacie. I thought you might be unhappy,' she confessed. 'I can see now, though, from all that you've said about your work, that you're more exhausted than unhappy. You're sure,' she added anxiously, 'that it's not too much for you?'

Kacie readily recalled the way she had scoffed at any suggestion that working for the chairman was more than she could handle. But with Elliot keeping up the pressure from first thing on Monday; by the time she staggered to her bed on Wednesday, she was of the view he was either working some devil out of his soul, or he was piling on the strain just to see how much she could take before she cracked.

By midday Thursday only pride prevented her from going to tell him he needed not one secretary, but six. Then, as she stood by one of the filing cabinets, Lana Neasom sauntered in. Jealousy dug a deep and painful furrow, so Kacie forgot all about Elliot's whip-cracking tendencies.

Elliot was up to his eyes with work, she knew. Apart from the paper work which flowed in and out all day, he was also busy tying up all loose ends before he left for Canada a week on Saturday. Scorched in her brain, however, was memory of his edict that Mrs Neasom could interrupt at any time. Which was why, when the blonde flicked her a snooty glance, and then began to amble towards his door, she made no move to stop her.

That passive stance did not suit the ill-mannered blonde either. For she was half way across the office carpet when she stopped and turned to raise a thin pencil-lined eyebrow in Kacie's direction.

'Don't you want to see my appointment card?' she questioned acidically.

A devil which had appeared in Kacie once before was suddenly there again, and would not stay down. She was aware that she should not let Lana Neasom's supercilious attitude irritate her, but that devil just refused to let her meekly take the woman's insolent arrogance.

'Feel free,' she drawled, and with a fine dismissive attitude, she waved her away with the back of her hand.

In a split second Kacie knew she would have been wiser not to have crossed her. For on the instant Lana Neasom's expression changed, making evident her fury at Kacie's insurrection. Her highly glossed lips twisted into a spiteful grimace.

'You tuppeny-ha'penny typist! Who *do* you think you're talking to?' she spat viciously.

She was shaken by the spite and spleen she saw in the heavily made-up face, but somehow, Kacie found she could not back down. She discovered she had a fine arrogance of her own.

Flicking a disdainful glance over the blonde, she replied, 'I'm not sure—*what*—it is.'

She was then more shocked than shaken; for such a string of foul abuse promptly hit her ears, she could only stare with horrified, incredulous eyes. Paling visibly at the names the woman called her, Kacie felt weak with incredulity that Lana Neasom, for all her refined appearance, should screech out such a volley of vile language.

Lana Neasom had still not finished when Elliot, disturbed by the commotion, came striding from his office. If he had seen Mrs Neasom in a temper before, or if he had not, it was straight away clear that he was not going to have such goings on in his premises.

His look from one to the other encompassed the shock in Kacie's face, while the blonde broke off her tirade to complain, 'Elliot this . . .'

He took a firm hold of Lana Neasom's arm, and pushed her, none too gently, towards the outer door. 'Take yourself, and your gutter language, off my property,' he let go furiously, then opened the door and with finality, he told her, 'And keep it that way.'

That she did not care to be thrown out of anywhere was obvious from the few foul epithets she aimed at Elliot before she went. The last words audible as he slammed the door on her were '. . . turn on me, just because your little virgin of a secretary won't let you touch her.'

Colour burning her face, Kacie turned her back to the door and tried for a 'business as usual' manner.

She had a shaking hand outstretched to the filing cabinet when Elliot came by her to go into his office. Abruptly he halted. As abruptly, her hand dropped to her side.

'I'm—sorry—about that,' he apologised grimly, when it was not his fault, but hers, she supposed, because she had provoked the blonde.

She wanted to tell him so, but he took a step nearer and scrutinised her flushed face, and her tongue just stuck to the roof of her mouth. Then her heart began to pump so energetically there was no chance for her high colour to fade. For suddenly she knew, when the language Lana Neasom had used was enough to make any but the most hardened blush, that Elliot was taking a double check on her crimson colour.

She had known all along that some time he would sift through what had taken place. But as she looked at him, Kacie saw that, too soon for her to have herself collected, Elliot had already done a quick flip back, and that he had just landed on the last thing Lana Neasom had said. Hastily, Kacie lowered her eyes.

'You're not ...' he rasped, his tone, his shock, telling her his had been a crashed landing into realisation. 'You—can't be!' he exclaimed, and plainly, he did not believe it.

Kacie had no intention of arguing with him. Instead she pulled open one of the drawers of the filing cabinet with no memory whatsoever of which file she wanted.

A hand coming to close the drawer shut stopped her. As she had known, Elliot had a mind which wanted to know how everything worked. He did not like mysteries. She knew he was determined to know the finer details of that which puzzled him when his hands gently gripped her arms, and he turned her to face him.

She tried to avoid his eyes, but was made to look at him when, still holding her with one hand, he tilted her head up with the other.

His expression was stern, she saw, but he was to confuse her thoroughly when, his question having nothing to do with anything that she could see, he grimly asked; 'Where, would you mind telling me, did you spend last weekend?'

'Not that it's anything to do with you,' she answered, trying to oppose the weakness his touch brought, with pretended aggression, 'but since you ask, I went to Wellsingham.' She would have left it there, only he continued to hold on to her, and to look at her with a steady grey eyed look that said he wanted more than that. 'It's near Straford-on-Avon,' he compelled her to add.

'Wellsingham. Is that where your family live?' he asked. He apparently remembered her telling him that her mother and stepfather lived near the Bard's birthplace.

'That's right,' she said, struggling in confusion to know what mystery that had, or had not, cleared up.

'Who is William?'

'My stepfather,' she replied. 'He rang last Friday and asked me to go home for the weekend because . . .' Her voice faded, bewildered when all of a sudden Elliot's stern expression fell away and, as if her heart had not enough to contend with, a slow and gentle smile suddenly broke from him.

'Oh Kacie, Kacie girl,' he said, and there was such a tenderness in those few words, that she thought she would faint from hearing it. 'Shyness. Shyness of the virgin you are. That's what got to you when you realised I could see—that night when you realised I was not blind to your lovely body, you . . .'

Screaming fear made her jerk away out of his hold.

There was no time to analyse any of what had been
said, all she knew was that they were on ground where
one wrong word might have him suspecting that she
had gone willingly to his bed, not from pity, but with
love.

'So now my guilty secret's out,' she said as
carelessly as she knew how. She took a step back, and
turned her attention once more to the filing cabinet.
'The Jackson Harper file,' she said in a voice that was
meant to imply she had more interest in work than in
this conversation. 'Now where . . .'

Without a word of warning, Elliot too took a step—
towards her. The next moment he had gathered her
into his arms.

On no, she inwardly groaned, he was just not
playing fair. More than anything did she want to lean
her head against his chest to savour this moment when
Elliot forgot to be the perfect swine he had been all
week. So great was her need of that comfort, she
almost gave in. The thistledown imprint of his lips
when he laid a gentle kiss on her cheek was something
she did not need in the war where one emotion battled
with rationality.

Fear that her weakness might make her reveal far
too much, won the day. Kacie was then searching for
every gram of flippancy when she pushed away from
him.

'Was that kiss my reward for being a good girl?' she
mocked carelessly. The hardening of his eyes showed
her that he neither cared for her mockery nor her
flippant attitude.

'You shouldn't need to cast your mind too far back
to remember you very nearly got much more than
that,' he retorted nastily, and turned to make his way
back to his office.

Hurt that he could refer so carelessly to what had

been beautiful for her, she fired up, 'The hazards of being a *female* secretary!'

He was good at slamming doors on her, she fumed, for that was the only answer she got. Damn him, she thought, and damn work, she rebelled, and went out to lunch.

Having left her office at a quarter to one, Kacie was back an hour later, but she was not in a happier frame of mind. Elliot was not yet back from his lunch, but it would have suited her just fine if he did not come back at all that afternoon.

On the dot of two, he strode in. Without a word or a glance, he carried straight on to his own domain.

Kacie came near to the end of her tether as the afternoon wore on. Elliot's orders were dished out in unfriendly curt and concise terms, and she complied while keeping any answer required to the most monosyllabic.

At five sharp, without bidding him good night, she covered her typewriter, and went home.

When she thought back over the day's events, she was positive she must have been crazy to have ever imagined a tenderness in his tones or to have imagined a gentleness in that brief kiss to her cheek.

By morning, Kacie had begun to be glad Elliot would shortly be going to North America. With her nerves becoming more ragged by the day, she considered she would need four weeks of not seeing him, in which to get herself back together again. With luck, by the time he returned, she should have got herself sorted out, and would be ready to act as his impersonal, personal secretary.

She was driving to work when she wondered why she should wait until he returned from his trip to begin her new campaign? Not that very much went on in the office that had anything to do with matters

other than business ... she then remembered
yesterday.

Well one thing was for sure, she determined as she
entered the building, there would be no discussion of
her virginity today. She had, hours ago, designated
Elliot's curiosity about where she had spent the
previous weekend, as nothing more than something
which had to be cleared out of the way in his summing
up as to whether or not she was a virgin. All too
obviously, when last Friday he had overheard her
arranging to spend the weekend with William, he had
thought William her lover.

With her backbone stiffened, Kacie decided she
would not give Elliot the chance to eavesdrop on any
of her private phone calls again. If any of her friends
rang, she would tell them they had rung at an
inconvenient time, and that she would ring them back
that evening.

She went into her office to find Elliot already at
work. But since it was more than likely that a grunt
would be all she received in answer to any good
morning she offered, she saved him the bother, and
started her working day without a word.

Kacie kept up her reserved front all the way
through dictation. But when office manners decreed
she addressed him in some form, instead of calling him
Elliot—which would probably have gone unnoticed—
she called him a more formal 'Mr Quantrell', and did
not miss the exasperated look he tossed her.

It was enough to tell her that his temper needed
only a small spark to ignite it. But her resolve was
armour-plated. The impersonal personal secretary was
what she was going to be; she was just not going to let
him get to her.

At least, that was the way it was supposed to go. But
she had not reckoned on being caught off her guard

when, later that morning, they were going through his
Canadian schedule.

By the look of it, she mused, he was going to meet
himself coming back if he accomplished all he had set
himself. For he had compressed his itinerary to accomo-
date three days in New York at the end, where he would
complete yet more negotiations. She could see he would
have all the administrative help he might need from
their Canadian division, but since they did not have an
office in New York, her concern made her forgetful of
her resolution to speak only when spoken to.

'You're going to acquire masses of paper work.' She
suddenly broke her vow of silence. 'Will there be
someone there to assist you in . . .?' Her words were
sliced off before she could utter them.

'If that was a hint you want to come to Canada with
me—forget it,' Elliot snarled nastily.

'I wasn't hinting anything of the sort,' she flared,
her reserved front shattered at his unfairness. She had
already known that he would be going without her,
and it hurt her pride that he could think she would
hint that she wanted to be taken along.

'I'm pleased to hear it,' he retorted, and did nothing
to cool the temperature, when he added, 'Away from
this office, you spell nothing but trouble.'

'How do I?' she challenged hotly, but knew before
he opened his mouth that she was going to get the
blame for Gavin Aitken's having taken a shine to her
in Paisley, and for Elliot forgetting his vow never
again to get involved with a female secretary in
his office.

Mutinously, she glared at him, then suddenly,
before Elliot could start to fire straight from the
shoulder, the phone shrilled. Kacie knew, when
instead of telling her to answer it, he picked it up
aggressively, that his patience was at a low ebb.

'Quantrell,' he said shortly into the mouthpiece, and looked as though he would slam it straight down again. Instead, with a barked command to make it quick, he passed the phone over, and she knew that if she did not want there to be repercussions, she had better do as he said.

'Hello Kacie, it's me, Vincent,' said a voice she remembered, if not the pathetic tone it now had.

'Hello,' she replied. Concerned by the note of misery in his voice she asked, 'Is everything all right?'

'Couldn't be worse,' he replied sadly. 'Julie has filed for a divorce.'

'Oh, Vincent,' said Kacie softly, but was sharply roused out of her sympathy when she caught Elliot's infuriated look.

She knew Vincent needed to talk some of his unhappiness out of his system. But if she did not end the call soon, she was going to get a ticking off from an increasingly impatient Elliot.

'Look, Vincent,' she said, conscious without having heard a word, that he had been talking, 'I'm a little busy right now. But . . .'

'I understand,' he sighed, and then suggested, 'You couldn't meet me after work, could you? We could have a drink at The Bell, and catch up on all the news.'

Kacie knew by then that 'all the news' would be an hour or so of her hearing all Vincent's troubles. With Elliot looking as if ready to blow a fuse, she was being pushed into a corner. 'I'll see you about six,' she told Vincent hurriedly.

Elliot was postively seething when she put the phone back on its cradle, and lost no time in taking a loaded swipe at her.

'So now we know,' he snarled, all aggression. 'Not content to have all the bachelors within a ten mile radius panting after you—you don't hesitate to date faithless husbands.'

With the greatest of difficulty, she hung grimly on to her temper. But since Elliot appeared to be waiting for some reply, it was with some degree of satisfaction, not to say saccharine, that she told him:

'For the purposes of getting the facts straight—Vincent is in the middle of a divorce.'

As soon as the words were out, she knew he had taken exception to her syrupy tone. He was hell-bent on having a go at her, she realised. The office was running comparatively smoothly, and so unable to use that as a catalyst to his rage it was her relationship with Vincent which became the reason for her receiving the full might of Elliot's wrath.

'My God!' he exploded. 'You're thinking to be the second Mrs Jenner?'

'Such thoughts,' she flared, not taking kindly to being bellowed at, 'have not been possible until now.'

'Do you love him?' he questioned fiercely.

Instinctively, she would have said a rapid 'No'. But as quick as that impulse was self-preservation and pride made her aware that it did not matter who she might say she loved, so long as Elliot did not know that he was the one who held her whole heart.

Strangely though, when she was ready to say that she did love Vincent, she found that her love was just something which she could not lie about. She was unable to answer, and attempted to change the subject.

'Shall we get on with some work?' she asked, her voice cool.

'Perhaps you'd prefer to work for a divorced man,' he grated. 'Perhaps, at last, we've come to the real reason why you left your previous employer—a married man.'

'I'm not sure I understand you,' she fenced. 'You know why I . . .'

'Advancement!' he scorned. 'Like hell. Your only reason for leaving Jenner was that you were in love with him—a man who already had a wife. You felt your old-fashioned virtues under threat when you learned that he was in love with you.'

Vincent was not in love with her, but that was beside the point. Elliot had made having old-fashioned virtues sound like a sin, and Kacie was wounded that he could throw his discovery of her virginity back at her as an insult.

'Maybe you're right,' she retorted now that the truth of her departure from Jenner Products, or as close the truth as he would get, was revealed.

To hear her confirm that she had lied at her interview and had in fact left her old firm because of her love for the man who ran it, did not lessen Elliot's ire. More furious than ever, his expression was murderous when he roared, 'Then *maybe*, now he's about to be no longer married, you have it in mind to return to his employ!'

An ice-cold hand took a grip on Kacie's heart. But even when she knew she was pushing her luck, she just could not resist answering, 'Anything has to be better than this.'

She'd gone too far. A granite mask came over his features. Shock hit her and it took her all her acting ability to conceal it.

His voice arctic, Elliot snarled, 'Far be if from me to stand in your way. I believe you know the way out.'

Stunned Kacie stared at him, her green eyes wide. Then, shocked, hurt, and humiliated, she gathered up what dignity he had left her with, and went proudly from his office. She paused at her desk to pick up her bag, then walked out of her office, out from the building, and out of a job.

CHAPTER NINE

KACIE had no memory of driving herself home that day. But the next morning, she was to re-live everything again and again. Her memories were punctuated with many a wishful 'if only'. If only she had kept quiet and had refused to be drawn.

Aimlessly she mooched around her flat, her mind on Elliot and how she had no office to go to on Monday. Never again would she feel that burst of adrenalin that had been activated from the moment of her first meeting with him. She felt flat and without purpose to know that their paths would never cross again.

If only Vincent had not phoned when he had. Though in all fairness, Elliot had been spoiling for a fight even before Vincent's call. What bug had been eating away at Elliot she had no clue—unless he was regretting the way he had turfed Lana Neasom out of the office the day before. Perhaps he laid the blame that he had lost himself a girlfriend at her door.

Abruptly Kacie turned her thoughts away from Elliot and his girlfriends, and she fastened her mind on how she had surfaced yesterday afternoon to remember that she was supposed to be meeting Vincent around six. She had been in no mood to sit sipping a Martini while she listened to Vincent pouring out his troubles. Though heard them she had, when she had phoned to cancel their arrangement. For Vincent in accepting she could not make it, went on to glumly tell her all his woes.

'I thought when Julie came back, she was all prepared to make a fresh start.'

'But—she wasn't?'

'This time she only came back to collect the rest of her things and to tell me what pieces of furniture she wanted from our home.'

Kacie reckoned things could not get more final than that. In despair herself, she felt every sympathy for him, and unable to help because she was fast learning that where the heart was concerned, one had to battle through on one's own. 'I'm sorry,' she sympathised.

'I had a letter from her solicitors this morning . . .'

Half an hour later, having given her chapter and verse of the break-up of his marriage, Vincent remembered he had some work he should be doing, but before he went, he asked:

'You don't mind if I ring you from time to time?'

'Of course I don't mind,' she replied. 'Only don't ring me at the office—it's not often I get a moment to come out from beneath the paper work.'

She came away from the phone knowing exactly why she had said nothing about losing her job. For one thing, it was all too recent a shock for her to be over her hurt and humiliation. For another, Vincent could well have offered her a job at Jenner Products. After working for a man like Elliot, Kacie knew she could not return to work for Vincent.

Her mother phoned on Sunday, and trying to keep her voice light and carefree, Kacie could not breathe a word to her about her instant dismissal.

After the most desolate weekend she had ever known, Monday came around and Kacie realised that, since she had to earn in order to eat, she should be doing something about looking for another job. But somehow, she could not find the will.

Common sense started to stir on Tuesday. Common sense—and indignation. Who did Elliot Quantrell think he was anyway? She would go out, right this

minute and buy a paper and find a job every bit as
stimulating as the work . . .

She was in the middle of wondering where she might
hope to find a job which afforded the same stimulation
her work for Elliot had given her, when the phone
rang. She went over and picked it up.

'Aren't you over the hump yet?' grated an
aggressive voice she would know anywhere.

Her heart raced, pounding an express train rhythm.
Kacie clutched at the nearest chair. 'I'm—not with
you,' she confessed, for in truth, just to hear him, had
her not knowing quite where she was.

'Which is precisely the point of my call,' Elliot
replied sharply. 'I need a secretary,' he went on curtly
and, even though he was no longer her employer, his
tone was as bossy as it had ever been. 'You're *it*,' he
told her, 'until I say differently. Get your car out
and . . .'

'My car's going nowhere!' Kacie cut in, her
indignation rising as she remembered her days and
nights of desolation and despair, and how only that
morning she had started to pull herself up by her
bootstraps. 'And,' she stubbornly added, 'neither am
I.'

'Don't be so bloody pig-headed,' Elliot rapped.

'Don't you swear at me!' she flared, but her anger
was already dying, her hate swinging abruptly to love.
'You finished bossing me around when you dismissed
me last Friday.'

'I . . .' he began, then halted. He seemed to have lost
his aggression, and she waited for him to go on, her
heart bumping. But now she was to wish she had not
waited. For it was not his aggression he had lost, but
his patience. Never a man to ask favours of anyone, he
let rip the cruellest words of all. 'Who needs you?' he
snarled, then slammed down his receiver.

Her intention to go searching for another job was forgotten that day. Prior to Elliot's call, she had deluded herself she was on the way to getting herself together. The fact he had telephoned and had said she was still his secretary, went a long way to heal the humiliation she had suffered. But that did not stop her from bleeding inside from the last three words he had spoken.

By Friday, she had again come to grips with herself. By then she knew it had to be for the best. It was far better the break should come now—yearn though she might to see him. For sanity's sake, she had to be strong. His cruel closing gibe still hurt, for he could not have stated more plainly that he did not need her at all. Anyway he would be off to Canada the next day. Telling herself that somebody out there must have need of her, she scanned the situations vacant columns.

Another grim weekend, with two job applications in the post, made her decide to make a determined effort to pick up the threads of her life. The badminton club had been sorely neglected of late, so for a start, although she could raise no enthusiasm for the game, she promised herself that she would go along there on Tuesday. Soon, she told herself, refusing to listen to that part of her which said differently, she would be back to the girl she had been before she had so disastrously fallen in love with Elliot.

On Wednesday Kacie received a telephone call from one of her job applications inviting her to go for an interview the next day. She agreed, thinking that to have short cut the postal system, the firm of Briggs and Mortimer must be in something of a hurry for a new secretary.

Her surmise proved correct when, having gone through the formalities of interview, she was offered the post, to start on Monday.

'Monday?' she questioned, knowing in her heart of hearts she did not want to work for Briggs and Mortimer.

'My previous secretary had to leave at short notice—a domestic matter,' Mr Russell replied, and asked, 'You *are* free to start on Monday?'

'Yes, of course.' She smiled, wondering why, since the only place she wanted to work was now closed to her, she had prevaricated.

'Good. I'll see you on Monday then.' He returned her smile, and escorted her to the door where he reminded her to bring with her her form P45 from her previous employer. 'Without it, you may find yourself paying emgergency tax,' he said on parting.

Kacie had not given a thought to her P45 form. But in bed that night she paused to briefly wonder why, when Quantrell Industries was such an efficient set up, they had not thought about it either. It will probably be in the post in the morning, she decided.

But there was nothing in the post on the next morning from Quantrell Industries. Around eleven o'clock, she decided to ring their personnel department.

'Kacie Peters here, Mr Owens,' she told him when she was put through. 'I'm calling to ask if you could send me my P45?'

'P45!' he repeated.

'I'm starting a new job on Monday, and . . .'

'You're leaving!'

'I've left,' she told him. 'I'm ringing from home. But I need . . .'

'You've left!' he exclaimed. 'But—I wasn't told . . . When did you leave? I've had no instruction from Mr Quantrell about you.'

'He must have forgotten . . .' said Kacie lamely, beginning to wish she had never telephoned.

'That's not like him,' Mr Owens told her, something which she already knew.

'We—er—had a deal to get through before he left for Canada. I expect a small thing like that slipped his mind.'

He did not sound convinced, but he assured her he would have the matter of her P45 attended to, and she rang off—puzzled. Why, she pondered, when Elliot knew she was not going back, had he not said anything to Mr Owens? Why, when the last time he had gone off to Canada he had instructed personnel to have a new secretary installed for when he returned; had he not done so this time?

She had given up trying to work it out, when a hour later a flustered Mr Owens rang back to ask had she and Mr Quantrell parted on amicable terms. Mystified as to the reason for his question, pride forbade she tell him anything of the way it had been.

'Mr Quantrell did ring after I'd left to enquire if I would come in to give a hand.' She dressed up the bossy phone call she had received.

'That's a relief,' he replied, and sounded as relieved as he said. Then went on to explain how he needed to search round for the right type of replacement for her, but that meantime, while the directors were in charge, could she come in to keep Mr Quantrell's paper work down in his absence.

'No I can't,' said Kacie promptly. Then because that sounded a little blunt, 'I'm sorry, Mr Owens, I can't,' she added, 'I've already . . .'

'It'll only be for a short while,' he urged, obviously in something of a flap. 'Apparently work is already piling up waiting for his return. Lord knows when Mr Quantrell will ever see his bed again if he has to come back and plough straight away into that lot.'

'I'm sure you can pull in someone from one of the

other offices,' said Kacie stoutly, weakening, but trying to tell herself it was no concern of hers if Elliot never saw his bed again. 'Who kept his paper work down the last time he went away?' she asked.

'One of the secretaries who swears that she'll never volunteer again. She went off sick the Friday before you started,' he told her. 'I'm trying to find someone who can cope without having a nervous breakdown ... you're the obvious choice, Kacie. *You* know the way Mr Quantrell works. You're familiar with the issues he had on the boil. As also,' he said, dropping his voice a confidential tone or two, 'you must be familiar with his recent illness.'

'Illness?' Kacie asked urgently, fear striking at her heart—until Mr Owens retracted.

'Well, not illness exactly. But in all the years I've been here, I've never known him have so much as a day off that wasn't connected with business or holiday. So the eye strain which kept him at home for a whole week, must have been pretty severe.'

'I didn't know anyone else knew about it,' said Kacie carefully, aware she knew more than Mr Owens about Elliot's eye strain.

'Mr Davy told me in confidence,' the personnel manager replied. 'But for all we know,' he went on whittling away her resistance, 'with a weakness established, Mr Quantrell may well suffer a return of the trouble.' What little resistance she had left, disappeared completely, when he added, 'You can just imagine the strain it will be on his eyes if he has to burn the midnight oil to catch up when he comes back.'

It was too late when she came off the phone to wish she had risked her neck and had asked Elliot the outcome of the Consultant's visit. The fear that he might again have to put up with being in that dark shuttered world—or worse—had made her promise to go into Quantrell Industries on Monday.

She then realised she would have to ring Mr Russell and tell him she had changed her mind about joining the firm of Briggs and Mortimer. She was loath to make the call, but since Mr Russell's need was so urgent, she could not see him being prepared to wait until she was finished with Quantrell's. She picked up the phone and dialled.

Kacie had the whole weekend in which to wonder, was she being a complete and utter fool? Elliot had told her how much he valued his sight, so was it likely, no matter how high the paper work was piled on his return, that he would take such a risk?

But, complete and utter fool or no, that persistent niggle of fear for his sight proved stronger than any argument she could raise to break her word to Mr Owens.

She drove to her old office on Monday glad that she had retained sufficient wit to remember Elliot's schedule. She had promised to work for three weeks only. When Elliot returned to his office three weeks today, she would not be there.

She went in to find Mr Owens had done his stuff, in that he had seconded a secretary who was to learn all she could, and who was prepared when Kacie left, to work on until a permanent secretary for Elliot was engaged.

Gail Turner was a pleasant young woman, recently married, and with no ambitions to further her career. Gail was doubly certain she had no career ambitions when, at the end of her first working day with Kacie, she came up for air, and exclaimed:

''Struth! If today was a sample of life at the top— they can keep it!'

'I felt pretty much the same on my first working day

with Mr Quantrell.' Kacie smiled. And not wanting Gail to be off to personnel first thing in the morning with a request to be moved, she encouraged her with a chirpy, 'It gets easier.'

'You reckon!' said Gail, her tone heavy with scepticism. 'There's so much to learn, and Mr Owens said you only promised to stay with me for three weeks.'

'We'll get through,' Kacie told her confidently. 'We had a backlog to tackle today which has made us behind. But you'll soon start to enjoy it.'

Gail did not look convinced, but she was a sunny soul. She appeared in the office the next morning—to Kacie's relief—and after a few moans about the weather, said, 'Right, now where in the middle of this Chinese puzzle, do you want me to start?'

They were going home on Friday when Gail, staggering to the door under the weight of her lunch time shopping, turned to accuse:

'You lied!'

'When did I?'

'You said it would get easier,' Gail replied, adding drily. 'It hasn't. Good night.'

Kacie grinned, and left the office only to bump into Jonathan Davy, who took the opportunity to ask her about the rumours he had heard about her leaving.

'Elliot accepted my resignation some time ago.' She evaded a direct answer, finding pride had made her every bit as good as the next person at pulling out the odd white lie.

'He spoke highly of your work,' Jonathan pressed, without knowing it taking the lead out of her shoes as she sailed heavenwards to hear, even at second-hand, Elliot's comments about her.

'I enjoyed my work,' she parried.

'So,' Jonathan sent her a charm filled smile, 'it must have been a personality clash?'

'Must dash,' said Kacie, her lips sealed on the subject.

'How about having dinner with me one night?' Jonathan suggested before he would let her go. 'We could maybe talk over what went wrong between you and Elliot. Maybe we could . . .'

'Really, Mr Davy,' Kacie told him, only one way out of this that she could see, 'you must know I was employed as a personal and *confidential* secretary.'

Promptly, his grin suggestive, 'I'm sure we could find something else to talk about,' he said lightly.

'I'm sure you could,' Kacie batted back, and left him with still an ample supply of other lines to try when next they bumped into each other.

By the middle of the second week, Gail and Kacie had settled into an orderly working pattern in which Kacie did most of the typing while Gail fielded any queries which came in, referring to her on the occasions when she was uncertain. With the aim of giving her experience of the wide variety of phone calls which frequently had to be deflected, the duty of answering the telephone was also handed over to Gail.

On Thursday, while Gail was out at the dentist's, a visit she would have been very happy to cancel, it was Kacie who, moving to the other desk, answered the phone when it rang.

'Goodness knows where Mr Glover or his secretary are,' gabbled a flustered switchboard operator in her ear. 'I'll put the call through to you.'

From the girl's unusually flustered manner, Kacie guessed someone important must be waiting—not very patiently either—for Cecil Glover to be run to earth. Then suddenly her heart gave such a lurch, that she physically flinched at it.

'At last!' grunted Elliot shortly. 'Cecil . . .'

'I . . . It's not . . . Mr Glover c-can't be traced at the moment,' Kacie interrupted, falling over her words.

The silence from the other end told her Elliot was about to hit the roof. But, to her immense surprise, when after a long pause his voice came again, she could have sworn that all aggression had gone from him. If anything, there seemed to be a touch of warmth in his tone, clearly recognising her voice, he said, 'This is a surprise.' Her voice caught somewhere in her throat at the unexpected warmth which suggested he was not angry to find her working in his office. 'I thought you might have returned to Jenner Products,' he added mildly.

'I—didn't,' she answered, desperately willing her brain to wake up and stop compelling her to tell him something so obvious.

'Instead,' Elliot picked up—and there was a smile in his voice if her ears weren't deceiving her—'you decided to return to work for me.'

'Well, not exactly,' she said chokily, her legs feeling like water, so that she just had to sit down. 'Mr Owens has co-opted me to brief the girl who's to fill in while he looks round for the right kind of permanent secretary for you.'

Kacie knew then, with Elliot all warmth and affability, that if he asked her to continue to be his permanent secretary, she would have no strength to resist the temptation.

But he asked no such thing. Instead, with that smile still in his voice, he merely murmured, 'Nobody briefed you, Kacie.'

'It won't take long,' she replied, and then recalled his words 'Who needs you' with painful clarity. A touch of coolness had entered her tone, when she told him, 'Mrs Turner is most capable—I'll stay with her one more week, then she'll be fine to work on her own.'

Elliot, it seemed, had not the slightest interest in Mrs Turner's capabilities. But there was a definite hardening in his attitude, when abruptly, he asked, 'You *do* intend to return to Jenner then?'

'It's—a possibility,' Kacie lied, and wanted quite desperately to hear him warm to her again.

But the earlier affability did not return, and he was back to being the old Elliot when, with underlying sarcasm, he took it upon himself to enquire, 'Love life's going smoothly is it?'

'Flourishing,' she tossed back, and seeing no reason why it should be one way traffic, 'How's yours?' she asked.

'I'm not getting enough sleep,' he replied, to make her wish she had never asked. On that unsatisfactory note, he ended his call.

Kacie spent the next ten minutes in the cloakroom reliving every word he had said, and trying to collect herself. Her insides were all tied up in knots. She hated herself for turning cool on him, for it was then that Elliot's voice had lost its warmth.

To start with, he had sounded as pleased to hear her voice as she had been to hear his—she was sure of it. If only she had not so stupidly remembered he had no need of her. If only . . .

Kacie took a grip on her thoughts, then gave herself a stern lecture. Of course Elliot would be pleased to hear her in his office—but only because she was most likely the best person to keep it smoothly ticking over while he was away.

She began to doubt there had been warmth in his voice at all, and her spirits sank to rock bottom when she realised just how tricky the imagination could be. His voice had only sounded warm because she had wanted it to. Pure imagination, she saw, had conjured up a warmth which quite obviously was no more than a distortion created by the mechanics of a transatlantic link-up.

She had been back at her desk for five minutes when suddenly into her depressed thoughts, the most astonishing realisation struck. Elliot had rung off without telling her why he had rung in the first place!

That wasn't like him! He was just not the type to waste valuable time making unnecessary telephone calls; not when he knew she was used to taking confidential messages and would take down, word-perfect, anything he wanted passing on to Cecil Glover!

Minutes passed as she pondered why—when she should forget work and everything connected with it the moment she heard his voice—Elliot, with his legendary memory, should similarly forget what he had rung for, on hearing her!

When eventually the unpalatable truth forced its way in, she did not want to believe it. But the truth was starkly obvious. Elliot no longer trusted her with confidential matters.

Her last ounce of self-confidence was gone; taken from her. She had wanted to believe that no matter what else happened between them, she still had Elliot's trust. To find that reality was to the contrary was a crippling blow.

She had still not surfaced from her self-denigration when Gail, much happier than when she went out, returned from her visit to the dentist.

'How did it go?' Kacie raised herself up from the depths of despair to enquire.

'My dentist's a magician.' Gail grinned. 'He only has to poke his head round the surgery door, and say "Come in, Mrs Turner", and I turn into a five-year-old child again.'

Kacie laughed, but tears were near.

For the remainder of her time at Quantrell Industries, she was reluctant to answer the telephone.

She knew she was being ridiculous, for she would have given anything to have Elliot ring through and ask her to take down a confidential message. But she knew he would not. As far as he was concerned, she had already left the firm. Nothing confidential to his Canadian trip was going to come her way.

It cost her dear to accept that Elliot no longer trusted her. Had it not been for the fact she had grown to like Gail and knew she would be upset if she walked out before her promised three weeks were up, Kacie would never have gone into the office again. But she stuck it out. She was happy when her last Friday arrived, and she was left with nothing more to do at Quantrell Industries, but to try and instil into her colleague some of the confidence she knew Gail was going to need when Elliot returned on Monday.

Kacie made her final departure from Quantrell Industries, heartily wishing she had never agreed to go back. The hurt inside was continuous torment, and the pain was just not getting any better.

On Saturday, as she had before, she made another attempt to pull herself together, only this time, it did not work. Without enthusiasm she bought a paper, but could not summon up the volition to look for another job.

Towards evening she thought about a vigorous game of badminton. The idea was rejected. Somehow she just could not face being a part of the hearty badminton group.

She took herself off to bed, and promised herself that she would make a greater effort in the morning— if morning ever arrived!

Kacie was still awake when at two o'clock, her telephone rang. More for something to do other than just lie there waiting for it to stop, she got out of bed. No civilised person rang up for a chat at such an ungodly hour, so she concluded that her caller must be some party reveller stabbing out the digits at random. Dully, she picked up the phone. Then, like someone waking from the dead, she promptly came to life.

'Fancy coming to the airport to pick me up?' Elliot, his voice gritty, and just a shade on edge, enquired.

Kacie had to wait a moment while she found a tone to counter the hurried beating of her heart. 'Have you any idea of what time it is?' she asked coldly.

'My flight was delayed by bad weather in New York,' he replied, to give her the impression that he thought no other explanation for getting her out of bed at two in the morning was required.

Love, Kacie discovered, could in one solitary instant, make her forget the whole terrible time she had spent since his last telephone call—if she let it.

'Too bad!' she snapped, drumming up every ounce of resistance.

'You—won't come?' Elliot asked, his voice suddenly flat, and not like Elliot's voice at all.

'Got it in one,' she forced out between her teeth. 'In the words of the immortal Bard, Elliot Quantrell, you can go and take a running . . .'

'Kacie,' He stopped her, an odd note of strain added to that flatness. 'Kacie,' he repeated, and then said clearly, 'I—need you, Kacie.'

Tears blinding her eyes, silently, she replaced her receiver. Oh, if only he had meant those words.

She was more wide awake than ever when she returned to her bed. But, when it was a choice between tears or mutiny, she chose the latter. Elliot did not need her—all he needed was a chauffeur. Who did he think he was anyway, ringing her up in the middle of the night?

For half an hour Kacie sat defying her heart, and railing against Elliot and his utter gall in thinking she would turn out of her nice warm bed at any hour he happened to land.

It wasn't as if he employed her any longer, she mutinied. Not like he had that other time when he had rung and told her to come and collect him from—the—air . . . port . . .

'Oh dear God, *no!*' she whispered aloud, and suddenly she was galvanised into action as she chased around getting dressed and finding her car keys.

By the time she was on her way, she was positive Elliot's eye trouble had returned. Supposing he was blind? she lashed herself as she drove along. How could she have spoken to him the way she had? Supposing he had taken her at her word and, although it would hurt his pride, had been forced to ask someone else to drive him to his home?

A fierce pride for him surged in Kacie then. A pride which decreed no one but she must drive him home. A pride of such proportions, it was unthinkable that anyone else but she should do it.

By the time she reached the airport, the jumble in her head had brought forth a couple of indisputable facts. The first was that Elliot must trust her after all. Whatever had made him forget to leave a message for Cecil Glover that time—Elliot would just not overcome his self-esteem and let someone witness a return of his affliction whom he did not trust.

The second, and painful, indisputable fact which came to her, was that she stood every chance of letting his trust down.

Oh, if only she had started out straight away, she anguished, as she raced up to the enquiry desk. What if she had missed him? What if, in the time it had taken her to get there, Elliot had already left?

CHAPTER TEN

ELLIOT had not gone. Directed to the annexe where he had waited once before, Kacie went on hurried feet, her agitation at a peak. Had Elliot, not wanting anyone to witness his blindness hidden himself away?

Her racing footsteps halted outside the door of the room where she knew him to be. A panicky breath choked her, and she took a moment to get her emotions under control. Fully aware he would not be able to see her, she still took another moment to compose her features. Then she opened the door, and went in.

As before, Elliot, tall and straight, stood with his back to her. In the grip of tenderness for him she realised that for all he must have heard her come in, his pride would not have him turn around lest she was a stranger.

Softly, she called his name. 'Elliot.'

She saw his broad shoulders move in a spasm of relief to hear her voice; to hear the voice of someone he knew. Then, slowly, he turned.

For a long, silent movement he stared at her with unseeing eyes, and said nothing. Then, his voice quiet, hushed almost, as though his aggression had been defeated by what had happened to him, he simply said, 'You—came.'

Emotion threatened to betray her. So badly then did she want to hold him close, and to use what words of comfort she could. But he would not like that. He wanted neither pity, nor sympathy, from anyone. Though as she looked into his tired grey eyes, there

was no way she could contain her concern that the
lighting in the room might not be good for his eyes.

'Shouldn't you be wearing dark glasses?' she gently
suggested.

Puzzlement showed on his brow, and her heart sank
that with everything so dark to him, it made little
difference now whether he wore dark glasses or not.

His voice was measured and his tone careful as he
replied, 'I've been going around with blinkered vision
for long enough, Kacie.'

Oh Elliot, my darling, her heart cried, his
impatience with this second visit of an affliction he
found hard to bear, typical of him. She knew,
however, that 'love' mixed in with sympathy, was
something he had no time for either.

'How long,' she quietly asked, 'have you been—like
this?'

That puzzled look was there again, but for a second
time, albeit slowly, he did not hedge from answering.
'It—all came together in the plane.'

Oh God, Kacie thought, panic taking great swipes at
her at the thought of his blindness coming upon
him so suddenly. Had there been a doctor on the flight?
Who had looked after him? Not that that was important
now. It was more important that she got him home.

'My car's not far away,' she told him, while at the
same time she quickly organised her thoughts along
the lines of calling out a doctor the moment she had
Elliot at Ashwith Court.

Her actions as speedy as her thoughts, she moved
forward with the intention of attempting to pick up his
oversized suitcase. But was then momentarily struck
dumb when Elliot stretched out a hand and found her
arm, and held her steady in front of him.

'I'm not going anywhere, Kacie—until I know, one
way or other, where we're at,' he said suddenly.

The touch of his hand on her arm was no aid to her ability to make any sense of his remark. 'Where we're at?' she repeated. Fresh sympathy broke in her when suddenly it dawned how totally disorientated he must be in his darkened world, and quietly, she told him, 'We're at the airport.'

'I know that,' he growled, the impatience she had long expected to see, showing through. His frustration about something or other exploded. Totally unexpectedly, he added, 'I'm not blind!'

Stunned, she opened her mouth, but no sound came. She made a second attempt. 'You're—not blind?' she asked faintly. Rapidly then, she began to come out of her shock, her voice starting to rise. 'There's nothing wrong with your sight?' she challenged.

'Of course, there isn't,' he confirmed. 'The problem I had before has cleared completely.' His expression then changed, and he had started to look fairly shocked himself, when, 'Surely you didn't think . . .' Angrily, Kacie cut him off.

'What else was I supposed to think,' she flared, all recent sympathy sent flying by the feeling she had been an idiot of the first order. Furiously she tore her arm from his grasp. 'You drag me from my bed in the middle of the night . . .' she raged, and would have raged some more but for a sudden movement from the man beside her.

'Oh, Kacie,' Elliot groaned. 'It's going all wrong before I get started.'

She was unable to understand his words, just as she was unable to understand why, when she had never known Elliot to show vulnerability about anything, he should look so utterly defeated now. But she was too furious with him, and with herself, to want to linger for enlightenment.

Swiftly she headed for the door. If he wanted a lift home—let him thumb it. With living proof that there was not a thing wrong with his eyes, as swiftly as she moved, Elliot was at the door before her.

'Let me by,' she ordered tartly.

'When you've heard what I have to say, and not before,' he grunted, more in the manner of the man she knew, than the man he had been when she had arrived.

'I assure you,' she arrogantly told him, 'that I'm not the *remotest* bit interested in anything you have to say.'

He did not like that, she saw. But the old Elliot was very much to the fore when he grabbed hold of her and pushed her unwilling frame down into a chair.

He stood over her, and grated, 'If you want to tell me that, when I've finished, then I'll—consider—accepting it. But first—even if I'm about to make one almighty fool of myself—you're going to hear me out.'

'You make a fool of yourself!' she gibed. 'That'll be the day!'

He gave her a tight-lipped look. Though oddly, when she had only ever known him to be supremely confident, there seemed more than a trace of uncertainty about him when, as if unsure where to begin, he paced away from her.

Kacie was still smarting, and love him though she might, she was in no frame of mind to try to help him out.

'Since you aren't going to let me out of that door until you're through,' she said tartly, 'would you mind getting on with it. I don't mean to be tiresome,' she offered sarcastically, 'but I wouldn't mind seeing my bed again—before daylight, if you have no objections.'

She flicked an uninviting glance to him, and was at her most unresponsive when he placed a chair opposite hers. But when, with his eyes never leaving her face, Elliot lowered his length into the chair, she suddenly started to grow wary. For it seemed to her then, that he had no intention whatsoever of missing any change of expression which might fleetingly stray over her features.

His eyes were still firmly fixed on her, when he began, 'These past weeks have been so filled with a multitude of meetings, of decision making, I've had no free time to give any deep consideration to ...' he paused briefly, then went on '... to a certain matter; which was constantly with me.'

Kacie saw at once that he had a problem which could not be dealt with by one of his instant decisions. What that problem was, however, or how it involved him making some kind of a fool of himself, was something which she could not see.

'You said,' she remembered, 'that it all came together on the plane. As you were not afflicted by a sudden attack of blindness,' she inserted sarcastically, 'can one assume you were referring to—a certain matter?'

Her sarcasm had not gone down well, she saw, but since she intended to show him her hardest front, Kacie told herself she did not care how much he scowled at her.

'I noticed you were smart on the uptake on the first day I saw you.' He swallowed his dislike of her sarcasm to reply civilly.

'Flattery will get you nowhere,' she told him waspishly, but felt her anger begin to fade when he bit back some sharp retort, and ignored her comment.

'It was only—when for once on a long flight I had no mind for paper work—that finding myself with more free time than I've had in ages, I sat back to let my thoughts wander.'

'Your—wandering thoughts,' she guessed, her sarcastic edge gone, 'gave you the answer to your problem?'

'I have to admit,' he replied, his alert eyes watchful on her face, 'in respect of—this issue—any power of clear analytical thinking I ever had, has been clouded of late.'

Surprise kept her silent for a second or two. Elliot's clear-headed thinking was phenomenal! Countless times she had seen him wade into impossible technical detail, turn it sideways, even stand it on its head, and then translate his conclusions into something that made sense.

'But—have you been able to reach a conclusion in this problem case?' she asked.

'While I was airborne, I thought I had,' he agreed. 'In fact, the conclusions I was able to draw then appeared so concrete, that the last hour of waiting to land was pure and absolute torment.' To her bewilderment, he then confessed, 'I'm still in torment, Kacie, because it seems to me now, that my—findings—could well be based on nothing more solid than quicksand.'

Kacie owned herself baffled. The Elliot she had worked for never had need for second thoughts on any matter. He had a first class logical mind; a mind where clouded thought just did not exist!

'You—er—obviously started at the very beginning,' she suggested, knowing that was the way his mind worked.

Briefly, he looked from her. Then, when he was just not the type to be nervous of anything, she had the oddest impression that he was exactly that. But, with a long indrawn breath he seemed to have taken a grip on himself, and his eyes were again fixed on hers.

'I've had hour upon hour in which to go over every

word, every look, every nuance,' he said quietly. In spite of herself her interest was sparked in the problem, as he continued, 'I went right back, not once, but many times, to the day I first set my eyes— on you.'

'On me!' she exclaimed. If she had any part to play, it could only be a minor one. 'You're talking of some matter of which I have knowledge,' she said more calmly. 'Some business I've assisted you——'

'This has nothing to do with business,' he cut in before she could finish. 'What I'm talking about,' he said, and paused before, deliberately, he went on, 'is the irrational person I became, the irrational person you made of me, within the first ten seconds of that meeting.'

Her initial reaction was one of disbelief. Then it penetrated that Elliot *had* said what she thought he had; and that he had brought the conversation from an impersonal to a personal level. She jerked upright.

'Irrational?' she queried. The hint of a curve on his mouth suggested he had observed her uncontrolled spasmodic movement and was encouraged by it. She tried to keep her wits about her as she went on, 'It isn't like you—to be irrational.'

'You don't have to tell me that,' he commented. 'But I don't know what other word I can use. When my first reaction was to show you the door—I found that I was marching down to personnel to get your file instead.'

Kacie did what she could to find a cool front.

'Why irrationality?' she asked, after a moment. 'Could it not have been your sense of fair play th...'

The shaking of his head told her he was sticking to his irrationality theory. The curve faded from his mouth, he made her work overtime to hang on to her adopted cool front, when he asked, 'Was it rational

that I should tell Jonathan Davy not to show his face
inside your office unless on a matter of business he
could not otherwise do on the internal phone?'

'You—didn't want him wasting your time?' she
asked, and without any idea of what the conversation
was now leading to, felt suddenly quite breathless.

'I didn't want him wasting *your* time,' he replied.

Elliot was obviously saying he had no room in his
Company for time-wasters.

'I was there to work,' she concurred stiffly.

'Which is exactly what I told myself when, again
irrationally, I became irritated when every day some
man or other would phone you.'

'Not every day!' she protested.

'It seemed like it,' he growled. 'I thought when I'd
sorted out Jonathan Davy and Mike Carey, that we'd
be left in peace with no more irritating interruptions. I
had not,' he went on ruefully, 'counted on the Simons,
the Anguses, and the Vincents of this world.'

'You left out the Gavins,' she reminded him huffily,
no nearer understanding what all this was about. She
was fast forming the view that—with nothing better to
do in the early hours of Sunday morning—Elliot
was of a mind to take her to task for past
misdemeanours. That she was sitting there taking it—
if she was honest with her heart—sprang from the
weakness that came from having not seen him for such
a dreadfully long time.

'I hadn't forgotten him, nor William either,' he told
her. 'Though it was on account of your friend Simon,
that I had reason to wonder what the hell was
happening to me.'

'Simon?' Kacie questioned, and wondered where
her smart-on-the-uptake streak was then, when, lost,
she queried, 'But—you don't know Simon?'

'I knew his name, just as I knew you had a date with

him on the night I made you work overtime. I also know the complete idiot I felt when, with that triumphant smile on your face, you told me that your date was not for that night.'

'You—made me work—that night—to prevent me—going out with Simon!' she gasped.

'I discovered a very possessive streak in myself—where you're concerned,' Elliot replied evenly. Kacie could only think he must mean he had an employer's possessiveness over a secretary's time. But he went on to leave her gaping at his next revelation. 'I felt a violent objection to your plans on overhearing you arranging to go away with him for the weekend. Which is why I decided that might be the very weekend to visit Dougal Aitken.'

'You . . .' Her voice failed. She tried again. 'You—decided *after* hearing me discuss the weekend with Simon, that we—you and I—should go to Scotland?'

'There was no great urgency for me to get to Paisley,' Elliot owned. 'Nor was there any real need, since contracts are purely the responsibility of the firm's legal department, for me to take you with me.' Her eyes large in her face, Kacie stared speechlessly at him, and he continued. 'If you need more proof of the sudden irrational person I had become; where once my schedule decreed it unthinkable I should take the time to drive all that way, it just didn't cross my mind to consider that I could make the trip quicker by air.'

Stunned by what she had heard, nothing entered Kacie's brain for a moment. Then all she could think to say, was a winded, 'But—I told you—before we got to Paisley—how my planned weekend away—was with Simon—and others, for a badminton tournament!'

'I've not forgotten a word of what you told me,' he confirmed. 'Which makes me seem irrational in the extreme, wouldn't you say, to be pleased by what you'd revealed, while at one and the same time, I was so disgruntled to know I'd made a fool of myself a second time, that I couldn't bear to talk to you.'

Her heart was palpitating wildly, but she had never forgotten that silent journey. 'You barely said another word until we reached Dougal's place,' she uttered weakly.

'Which was when my possessive streak revealed itself, when Aitken's son asked us to stay to dinner, wanting to get you on his own. I couldn't allow it.'

'You didn't—seem to care for it when I smiled at him either,' Kacie chokily recalled.

'No,' he agreed. 'Only to find myself feeling bereft at the hotel when there was no way could I tease that beautiful smile out of you, myself.'

A smile almost broke from her then. But, with her heart beating painfully against her ribs, other memories awoke; and suddenly she knew it was more than time she did something about getting herself together.

Her smile was still in hiding when to refresh his memory, she said, 'I didn't see much sign of you being bereft when you started to accuse me of making it with the hotel manager.'

'I didn't accuse without getting handsomely paid, did I?' he asked, a hand moving reminiscently to the side of his face which had felt the full force of her right hand.

'You—asked for it,' she mumbled, her heart hammering as she recalled the kiss which had followed. She saw his eyes go to her mouth, and knew that Elliot too, was remembering that moment.

His glance held hers again, steady and unwavering, when he said, 'I knew, when I kissed you, that you, dear Kacie, had got beneath my skin.'

'Oh!' she said startled, his endearment sending

shock waves through her. Then her throat dried so completely, that even had she been capable of forming any reply, no sound would have come out.

'That night, through the long wakeful hours,' he went on when she had nothing to add to her shaken gasp of surprise, 'I knew it wasn't only a feeling of possessiveness which had surfaced in me.'

'It—wasn't?' she asked, to be promptly staggered, when looking straight into her eyes, he continued with his explanation.

'Jealousy, is too small a word, Kacie, for the agony of mind I've been through.'

'Jealousy?' she questioned, her voice hushed. 'You w-were—jealous—over *me*!' Then because she just could not believe he meant what she would very much have liked him to mean, she quickly added, 'You mean you felt—something akin to the jealousy—some employers feel about lending their secretaries out?'

'Didn't you hear me, when I said that this has nothing to do with business?'

A sudden trembling started up inside her at what he had just said. To hear that his jealousy had nothing to do with business; that he had known an agony of mind, where she, personally, was concerned; was so earth-shaking that she just had to use what little intelligence he had left her with, to question his statement. To let herself believe what was so unbelievable was a high risk that could result in her hitting the ground with an almighty cruel crash if, for some heartless reason of his own, Elliot was just stringing her along.

'You...' she finally managed after seconds of saying nothing, '... you didn't ... That is, as I remember it, that next morning at the hotel—you didn't act very much...' She broke off, what she was trying to say swam confusedly in her head. 'You were in a foul mood the next morning,' she said, and left it at that.

'How else could I be?' he asked. 'I'd been determined at the outset that under no circumstances was I ever going to become involved. As I saw it then, there was no room for mixing business with pleasure.'

Her heart steadied down to a near normal beat. That said it all, she thought. Though the fact that she was still there, and that Elliot, with his watchful gaze still on her, did not appear to feel any great urgency to move, made her want a few crumbs of comfort.

'I appreciate your business means too much to you for you to allow yourself to become involved with a secretary who might turn traitor at a later date.' Then Kacie found the courage she wanted, to ask, 'But are you saying, that you felt—some emotion—for me?'

'What I'm saying,' he replied gravely, 'is that, since knowing you, emotions I've never known before, have stirred within me.'

'P-possessiveness—and jealousy?' She could not refrain from wanting him to re-endorse.

'Plus many others.' He momentarily salved her unrequited love. 'I could barely recognise myself in the bad-tempered brute you made of me,' he went on, taking the gilt from his previous statement. 'In my foul mood, I was determined not to let you get to me,' he admitted. 'Then you went sick with a heavy cold, and I couldn't stop thinking of how you lived alone and had no one to care for you. My determination to be aloof fell by the wayside and in my concern, I had to come and see how you were.'

Her emotions jerked up and down like some yo-yo on a string in his control. Every bit of intelligence told Kacie not to pursue, not to press for more, yet she found she just had to ask the question:

'You . . .' her voice faded, and she swallowed nervously, '. . . cared?' she brought out on a whisper.

'I wasn't ready to admit it,' he confessed, the intimation behind his words enough to make her feel giddy. 'But, out of the same concern, I was all set to call on you the next night too. That was before I rang and learned you weren't going short on male callers, or Chinese food.'

'H . . . His name was Sue,' she stammered.

Something seemed to crack inside Elliot then. 'Oh God,' broke from him, and he reached forward to take hold of her hands. 'Help me, Kacie,' he said, and his hands were gripping tightly on to hers, when he urged, 'For God's sake help me. I've been in one hell of a sweat ever since you walked in through that door—I just can't take——'

'What do you want me to do?' she swiftly butted in, her agitation getting the better of her. 'What—can't you take?'

'The waiting,' he replied tensely. 'Up there, on the plane, I thought I'd got everything documented in my mind. As we came in to land, I knew how—if I could get you here—it was all going to go. But,' he went on, a pulse starting to throb in his temple, 'for the first time in my life, I just can't wait until I have all the answers, and have given you all you need, before you tell me of an outcome which might go for or against me.'

'I'm not sure—what you're asking,' she said, and was not at all surprised her voice came out sounding shaky.

'I'm asking,' he said, and took another deeply drawn breath, then seemed to change his mind. 'I need to know what Vincent Jenner is to you.'

'Vincent!' she exclaimed.

'*Are* you in love with him?' Elliot asked. 'You gave

me the impression you were,' he pressed on as fear at telling the truth kept Kacie silent. 'But it wasn't until, on that flight, when I found my mind picking away at one or two incidents, that I began to query that impression.'

She made an instinctive move to pull her hands out of his grip. Then knew she would have done better to let her hands stay passively in his. For his look had sharpened, and his eyes refused to let hers look away.

'I've been at pains not to become one of your herd of admirers, Kacie. I got down to satisfactorily eliminating each one as not meaning very much to you, but when I was left with only Jenner, I came unstuck.'

'You—er—you seem—to have been—very busy,' she mumbled.

'I didn't stop there,' he replied, which was small comfort to her. 'But even as I looked for further proof of whether you loved him, it suddenly struck me as odd that you hadn't gone back to work for him.'

'He already had another secretary,' Kacie put in quickly, but the sceptical look, fleeting though it was, which crossed Elliot's face, told her she could have spared her breath. He was as aware as she, that Vincent could have found her a job, had she wanted to go back.

'Which in turn,' Elliot glided over her interruption, 'led me to consider just how close the two of you really were?'

Panic urged her to impress on him that she and Vincent were very close. Yet she knew that with Elliot digging and digging away he might soon remove the shield of her being in love with Vincent, so she stayed mute.

'Could you, I then asked myself, be in love with him and yet still be the way you had once been with me?'

Her mouth dry, her hands gripping his this time, Kacie stared and felt an almost irresistible urge to run. But Elliot gave her no chance to go anywhere. For with barely a pause, he was telling her the conclusions which had come to him.

'Your high moral standards might, I thought, prevent you from going to bed with him while he was still married. But, bearing in mind those moral standards, was it likely that you'd be as willing to go to bed with me as you were—if you were in love with some other man? Would you in fact, Kacie, go to bed at all, with a man you did not love?'

'I ... You ...' She had no hope of getting started, and no hope at all of finding an evasive answer. 'Look at the time!' she exclaimed, taking a glance at her watch, but not really seeing the dial. 'You must be out on your feet, Elliot. Jet lagged, and ...'

'Was it pity,' he cut in, 'which made you so willing to be mine that night? You infuriated me by shattering what I felt to be the most wonderful experience I'd ever known. Was it pity, or was it——'

'Good grief, Elliot.' Kacie, in utter panic, jumped in, though with no idea what to say next. For her part she found it shattering to hear him say that what had been so beautiful for her, had been wonderful for him! 'Nothing happened,' she said, her voice quick in her panic, and nowhere near as off-hand as she had tried to make it, 'so what does it matter? I've ...'

'Kacie Peters,' Elliot sliced in sternly, 'I recently stepped from a flight during which some answers about you brought such hope that it was unthinkable that I should land—be so near to you and yet so far—and not do something about finding out the truth.'

'You had to ring me in the middle of the——' She didn't get to finish.

'Regardless of the hour, I had to see you,' he told

her sternly. Then that stern tone faded, and as an
almost gentle note came to his voice, 'I had to see
you,' he repeated, 'because it seemed to me—if I'd got
it right—that you must love me . . .' Kacie jerked once
in his hold, and then froze, '. . . as I,' he added, 'love
you with all my heart.'

Her emotions in an uproar, scarlet colour surged to
her face. Incapable of speech, all she could do was to
stare at him while a desperate struggle went on inside
her. She ached to believe him, but the thought that he
should love her was too incredible.

As her initial sensation of shock faded, so she
perceived that this was no game Elliot was playing for
reasons too mysterious for her to fathom. As her green
eyes stared at him, she began to comprehend the strain
in his face.

Strain, and apprehension to know what her answer
would be, were both there in that gritted chin, and in
the tight mouth that spoke of an unbearable tension
within. She saw his eyes were hard no longer as they
searched into hers. Suddenly she saw torment in his
face, an agony that pleaded to know, had he got it
right, did she love him?

'You—love me?' Her voice was jerky, croaky, and
sounded not like her voice at all.

'More than I knew,' he answered. 'More than I
thought possible,' he said, his eyes fast on hers. Only
when he took another deep drawn breath, did Kacie
realise how hard he was striving to hang on to his
control. 'Have I deluded myself totally?' he questioned
tensely. 'Have I, in my summing up, been too clever
for my own good?'

'I—wouldn't say that, Elliot,' she said huskily, and
then—she smiled. 'In fact,' she told him, 'as usual,
you've got it right.'

'You—love me?' He returned her question, still

unwilling to relax yet; if he had seen her smile, then no answering smile was coming from him.

'Oh, yes,' said Kacie, 'I love you.'

'Then will you please tell me,' he breathed, 'what the hell you're doing sitting over there, when you should be over here?'

'Bossy brute,' she said softly, and laughed in utter joy at the moment when Elliot moved and brought her to sit on his lap.

'Let me hold you,' he said throatily. 'After the torment I've been through—just let me hold you.'

For how long he held her tightly to him, Kacie could not have said. All she was conscious of, as he held her in his arms as if he never intended to let her go, was the solace his embrace afforded.

With his face alongside her own, Elliot said not a word. It was as if the knowledge that she loved him was all he needed to comprehend. Then a shuddery sort of sigh left him, and he moved to look down into her face.

'I needed that,' he said, and then he kissed her.

Minutes ticked by as Kacie, with her arms wrapped around him, responded to her heart's impulse. Kiss for kiss she gave him, so that when they finally broke apart, her cheeks were again flushed—this time from another kind of emotion which he had stirred in her.

'My precious virgin,' he said tenderly, his warm grey eyes taking in her heightened colour. 'Were it not for an attack of shyness when you knew I could see, would you have been mine from love—not pity—that night you came charging into my room?'

'It was love,' Kacie confirmed simply. With unexpected shyness she hurried to add, 'After I heard that terrifying crash, it was panic that you'd hurt yourself that had me racing to you, more than anything.'

Lovingly he kissed the corner of her mouth. 'Is it any wonder,' he asked, 'with my head so full of you, I should absent-mindedly send that lamp crashing?'

'You were thinking of me?'

'I couldn't get you off my mind,' he told her with a quirky smile. 'We'd spent a lovely evening dining together, and I was facing the fact that I had something of a battle on my hands . . . I just wasn't concentrating on what I was doing then I knocked over the lamp and Lord knows what else. The next thing I knew, you were flying into the room looking like some sex-goddess with your shirt very near undone to your waist, yet at the same time looking so strangely innocent. Even then it didn't dawn on me exactly how innocent you were.'

'In my panic I forgot I was in the middle of getting ready to go to bed,' she murmured.

'I so nearly had you in mine,' Elliot said softly, then told her. 'I thought you were absolutely beautiful, and I knew I had to find some willpower. When I went to push you away, no sooner did I feel your hands in mine, than my resistance folded.'

'Oh Elliot,' she sighed blissfully. It had been exactly the same for her.

Kacie,' he murmured, and bent his head to her inviting mouth. 'I love you so, my sweet love,' he whispered as his lips left hers. 'I knew I was in love with you that night,' he said, his voice a caress. 'Which is why I was so enraged,' he pulled back to gently explain, 'when, about to share the pleasure of what I'd imagined was a mutual love that would make our lovemaking so very special for me—I was suddenly made aware you were not giving yourself out of love—but out of pity.'

'It wasn't imagined,' Kacie told him softly, and saw for herself the heartfelt joy it brought him to know there *had* been love in her response that night. Then suddenly, as it hit her, 'You knew you loved me *then*!' she exclaimed startled.

'I'd known since that afternoon,' Elliot confessed. 'We'd been out for some air, and had fallen in the snow. You had described the scene and I had grown more and more enchanted by your voice. I must have been half way to my discovery,' he said warmly, 'when over we went, and suddenly, when I found I wanted to hold you, and to just go on and on holding you, I knew then that I was in love with you.'

Dreamily, Kacie sighed, and as she remembered, 'Did you kiss me?' she asked.

'Only lightly. I just couldn't resist it.' He smiled. 'I couldn't believe that such an unwanted emotion had crept up on me, I was at once bombarded by thoughts of the string of men you had at your feet. I knew then I had to get back to the house to try to regain some sanity. I dared not,' he tenderly told her, 'give in to the overwhelming impulse to keep you in my arms.'

Simply because *she* could not resist it, Kacie stretched up to kiss him. Her rapture increased as his arms tightened around her and Elliot kissed her long and thoroughly. Though it was he who drew back, the love look in his eyes was such that she thought she might cry from pure happiness. Moments passed before she even vaguely remembered the conversation they were sharing before she had reached up to kiss him.

She found her voice from a throat choked with emotion. 'Did you—er—find the sanity you were looking for—when we returned to the house?'

'Not until I thought you were making love with me out of pity, did I come to my senses. But—even then—I hesitated to cut you out of my life.'

'You sacked me,' she reminded him, her humiliation of that time no longer significant.

'It wasn't thought out in advance,' he informed her gently. 'You'd just made me as jealous by intimating you were in love with Jenner. When you went on to intimate you'd like it better working with him than with me, black ice clutched my heart—the words seemed to say themselves.'

'Oh, darling,' she cried, anguished at the thought that, if she had been hurt by him, she had, in turn, caused him hurt. Again their lips met, but this time when his mouth left hers, it was he who remembered what they had been talking of.

After a pause, his caress on her face making her tremble, he resumed, 'Of course, I told myself I was glad I wouldn't see you again. But a weekend of you coming between me and my concentration, followed by a Monday of aching for the sight of you saw Tuesday arrive with me picking up the phone to ring you.'

'You—weren't very polite,' she teased.

'How could I be anything other than tough?' he asked, and, with a self-deprecating grin, 'I, who had always thought I was too strong to give in to such weakness!' Kacie thrilled to see him grin and to be free to enjoy his wry humour. Though he was serious when he continued, 'I felt I had made a fool of myself again and rang off in foolish pride. I really tried to make myself hate you during the rest of the week. I went to Canada still trying to get you out of my head and my whole system.'

'You rang off saying "Who needs you",' said Kacie, and confessed, 'Those three words devastated me.'

'Oh, Kacie,' he breathed in remorse, and gathered her close. 'I need you, girl,' he said emotionally. 'I need you.' He held her close to him and then told her, 'I needed you with me the whole time I was away. My need for you became an obsession. So much so, that when I put a call through to Cecil Glover and found you on the line instead, I was so stunned, so overjoyed to hear your voice, I entirely forgot the purpose of my call.'

'Oh!' she gasped. 'And there was I, crucified by thoughts that you hadn't left a message for Cecil Glover, because you didn't trust me. You normally never forget anything.'

'Good God!' he exclaimed, so startled it was obvious to her that such a thought as not trusting her, had never entered his mind.

'I'm sorry,' she said, feeling suddenly guilty to have ever had such thoughts.

'So you should be,' Elliot told her with a mock frown. 'Though some good did come out of that phone call.'

'You—felt better after it?' she queried.

'I wouldn't say that,' he replied. 'But on the plane the memory of that call, and how you had returned to the office in my absence, but had shown a decided aversion to returning while I was there, triggered off a succession of other thoughts.'

'The thoughts which brought you to the conclusion that I might be in love with you?'

He nodded, but revealed, 'I couldn't make any sense of my first question, though it did lead to the thought that since you should by then be working for Jenner, but weren't—were you perhaps, like me, behaving in an opposite way from the way you felt; as some sort of cover up.'

'You decided I might be?' she smiled.

'By the end of that flight I knew I couldn't wait to find out,' he answered. 'When my plane at last came in to land, I'd decided if I could get you to come to the airport to pick me up—since you were no longer on the firm's payroll and could just as easily thumb your nose at me if you wished—then surely I must mean something to you.'

'I wasn't going to come,' Kacie told him. 'I wasted all of half an hour convincing myself of that. That was before I had the panicky thought that your sight had gone again.'

'For whatever reason, you came,' he said softly, satisfaction there in his voice. 'Though not before I had begun to suffer the acrid taste of defeat.'

'You thought I wasn't coming?'

'You took so long to get here,' he said. 'I was on the point of having to accept you felt nothing for me, when I heard hurried footsteps coming this way. I felt such an upsurge of emotion that, though I wanted to run to the door and haul you in, I had to turn my back. I needed to steady myself, needed to get some sort of control. For in truth, my dear love, I didn't know how I was going to face the bitter disappointment, if those flying footsteps were not yours.'

Who kissed whom then, Kacie did not know. But when they broke apart, what she did know was that he was still not clear of the jealousy he had felt over Vincent.

His look thoughtful, Elliot stroked a caressing finger down the bridge of her nose, and then, quietly, asked, 'Were you ever in love with Jenner?'

She hesitated, but that honesty in her would not have her evading the question—not now she knew Elliot loved her.

'I—He . . . As you so quickly guessed, my reasons for leaving Jenner Products were not quite as I stated at my interview,' she began after a slightly faulty start. 'Though I'm still not sure, unless it was from some mixed up feeling of self-preservation, why I asked that stupid question at my second interview as to whether you were married. I thought I was in love with

Vincent,' she owned, then when she saw what it was doing to Elliot to hear that, she hurried on. 'I soon discovered, however, that what I felt for him was not love, but plain simple affection and sympathy. He's a kind man,' she explained, 'and often needed a sympathetic ear when the problems in his marriage became more than he could bear.'

'You said,' Elliot back tracked, when he had silently heard her out, 'that you soon discovered you didn't love him?'

Kacie relaxed, and rejoiced to know she had no need to have secrets from Elliot any more. 'If you're fishing, Mr Quantrell,' she teased, 'then I'll tell you that I started to think less and less about Vincent, on the day I met you.' Her teasing manner had gone, however, when she told him, 'I knew, when Lana Neasom, throwing her "darlings" at you right, left and centre, walked in that first time, what being *really* in love felt like. What being torn apart by gut-wrenching jealousy felt like.'

'Oh, my dear beloved,' he breathed tenderly, 'you've loved me from as far back as then! You were jeal——' He broke off, and his expression was never more serious when he told her how Lana Neasom meant nothing to him. 'You've no need to be jealous, sweet Kacie.' Then he said apologetically, 'Believe me, I'd no idea that woman, whom you pegged at once as no lady, possessed such a disgusting mouth.'

Kacie confessed, 'I'm afraid I provoked her outburst by being a shade unladylike myself. Well,' she amended at his look of doubting that statement, 'she didn't like it when, as if I wasn't the least bit jealous of her, I waved her into your office. Things went rapidly downhill from there.' The palest tinge of jealousy lingered still, when Kacie added, 'I lost you a girlfriend.'

'We were never as close as I made you believe,' he did not hesitate to tell her. 'In fact I'd forgotten her existence until I had to contend with sour thoughts of some male 'take-away' fiend monopolising the time I wanted with you. I'd already given Gavin Aitken a flea in his ear when he rang to try and worm your address out of me and the first sight I had of you when you returned to work from your cold, was of you flirting in the corridors with Jonathan Davy.'

'Flirting?' she queried gently.

'That was the way it seemed to me,' Elliot growled. 'You'd got to me Kacie,' he admitted, 'and I didn't like it. Nor did I like the thought that you knew I was attracted to you. You must have seen,' he inserted, 'how very desperately I wanted to kiss you when I was putting your pillows right at your flat. I rang Lana Neasom with one view only in mind. No way, I vowed, was my name going to be added to your list of lovers. It was high time, I thought, you should know I had other fish to fry.'

Kacie laughed, and murmured, all jealousy dead and buried, 'Er—I don't have a list of lovers.'

'Which is just as well,' she was informed. 'From now on, sweetheart, there'll be no room for the rest of the herd. Men are always going to admire your beauty, I know that,' he acknowledged, 'but from now on, my ring on your finger will make sure they admire you from a very long way off.'

'Your ring!' Her heartbeats were suddenly all out of rhythm again. 'W-we're—you mean—we're getting *engaged*?'

'We're getting *married*,' he told her, brooking no refusal. 'For the sake of my peace of mind, the sooner the better.'

'But you don't want to be married! You said you'd seen . . .'

'A bachelor's last stand,' he interrupted unblinking. 'You'll forgive me that, I hope, after all I've been through.'

'I'll forgive you anything,' Kacie beamed, 'and be delighted to take your bachelorhood from you.'

'Wretched women,' he said lovingly, and kissed her. Then with that kiss not enough, he kissed her again more deeply, and kissed her yet again. Passion soon flamed into life, Elliot's ardent caresses leaving Kacie ready for more. At last he moved back.

'In the interests of my blood pressure, I suggest we get out of here.'

Kacie gave him a bemused smile, and he hefted up his luggage and took her with him to the door. But before they went through that door, with so much said; with so much open-hearted honesty having passed between them; she suddenly halted. She knew she would not rest until she had confessed. Elliot halted with her, his look questioning.

'Elliot—I haven't been totally honest with you.'

'you—haven't?' he quieried, a mask coming over his features as though, it being too soon for him to be entirely sure of her love, he was bracing himself for the biggest let-down of his life.

'That time at Ashwith Court,' she said quickly. 'That day—when I couldn't leave because we were snowed in—well, I could—leave I mean. The snowplough had been along . . .'

A pent-up breath left him. Then suddenly his grin broke free. 'I know,' he said.

'You know!'

'I could see enough to know there was no snow on the road outside,' he owned, her dumbfounded expression delighting him. 'That was another of my questions. Why, I asked, when I'd worked with you for long enough to have seen your honesty and integrity, had you not after that one attempt—which I'd hastened to cut short—found another opportunity to tell me there was no need for you to stay the night. Could it be that you wanted to stay at Ashwith, as much as I didn't want you to leave?'

'You wanted me to stay!'

'Naturally I found other reasons for wanting you there,' he said with dry humour. 'I was bored with having to endure putting drops in every four hours. Bored with having the simple pleasure of being able to read taken from me. My excuses,' he owned, 'were endless. I'd just been poleaxed to realise I was in love with you, remember.'

'You tried to pretend it hadn't happened?'

'It wasn't easy coming to terms with a love I thought would never be returned,' Elliot said gently. Then, just as gently, he asked, 'Did you want to stay that night at Ashwith, Kacie?'

'Yes,' she said, and smiled.

'Would you settle for another visit—very soon to be a more permanent visit—as quickly as I can get you there?'

'Yes,' she said again, and laughed from sheer joy of the way he made her feel.

'Come on then,' he said, and with one arm around her, he escorted her from the room.

They were on the outside of the airport building when she went to go one way, and he went to go another, and they both halted.

'My car's this way,' Kacie told him.

'We'll get there faster in mine,' he said, and his arm possessive about her, he led her in the direction he had been heading.

'Elliot Quantrell!' Her severe exclamation—as it dawned on her that his car had been parked in the long stay car park the whole time—stopped him.

He looked down at her, the wicked grin on his face making her heart turn over. The look of love in his eyes when, regardless of who was about, he bent his head to kiss her, was enough to melt her bones.

'Love me?' he asked softly.

Kacie, her heart shining in her eyes, nodded. Willingly, she went wherever he led.

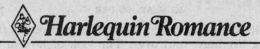
Harlequin Romance

Coming Next Month

2803 A THOUSAND ROSES Bethany Campbell
The tough-talking daughter of a professional wrestler isn't
intimidated by a miserly Scrooge who tries to lay claim to her
home at Christmas. But the strange tantalizing force drawing
them together unnerves her.

2804 THE HERON QUEST Charlotte Lamb
For a writer and a TV producer who set out to make a
documentary together, love isn't out of the question. But
according to him, marriage is....

2805 AT DAGGERS DRAWN Margaret Mayo
A surgery nurse has a rough time convincing her new boss in
the Lake District that she didn't take the job to be near his
brother. Then when she does convince him, an old boyfriend
turns up and ruins her hopes of marriage.

2806 CAPTURE A SHADOW Leigh Michaels
When a New York editor's top-selling romance author quits,
she sets off on a frantic search with only a pen name and a
Midwest town post-office box to go on. Luckily, an
outrageously appealing local author joins the hunt.

2807 THE WAITING MAN Jeneth Murrey
A widow and her son, heir to the family fortune, are tracked
down by her grandfather's handsome henchman. He has his
own ax to grind with her tyrannical grandfather. But is
marriage the answer?

2808 TWO WEEKS TO REMEMBER Betty Neels
If two weeks could turn into a lifetime, then a typist would
have more than memories of her thrilling trip to Norway with a
brilliant doctor. She'd have a bright, shining future as his wife!

Available in December wherever paperback books are sold,
or through Harlequin Reader Service.

In the U.S.
P.O. Box 1397
Buffalo, N.Y.
14240-1397

In Canada
P.O. Box 603
Fort Erie, Ontario
L2A 9Z9

Six exciting series for you every month... from Harlequin

Harlequin Romance·
The series that started it all

Tender, captivating and heartwarming...
love stories that sweep you off to faraway places
and delight you with the magic of love.

◆

Harlequin Presents·
Powerful contemporary love stories...as individual as the women who read them

The No. 1 romance series...
exciting love stories for you, the woman of today...
a rare blend of passion and dramatic realism.

◆

Harlequin Superromance®
It's more than romance...
it's Harlequin Superromance

A sophisticated, contemporary romance-fiction
series, providing you with a longer,
more involving read...a richer mix of complex plots,
realism and adventure.